IN TOO DEEP

IN TOO DEEP

A ROBYN HUNTER MYSTERY

NORAH McCLINTOCK

MINNEAPOLIS

First U.S. edition published in 2013 by Lerner Publishing Group, Inc.

Darby Creek
A division of Lerner Publishing Group, Inc.
241 First Avenue North
Minneapolis, MN 55401 U.S.A.

Website address: www.lernerbooks.com

The images in this book are used with the permission of: Front
cover: © iStockphoto.com/Kuzma.

Main body text set in Janson Text Lt Std 11.5/15.
Typeface provided by Linotype AG.

Library of Congress Cataloging-in-Publication Data

McClintock, Norah.
    In too deep / Norah McClintock. — 1st U.S. ed.
        p.   cm. — (Robyn Hunter mysteries ; #8)
    ISBN 978–0–7613–8318–5 (lib. bdg. : alk. paper)
    [1. Mystery and detective stories. 2. Group homes—Fiction.
3. Juvenile delinquency—Fiction.] I. Title.
PZ7.M478414184In 2013
[Fic]—dc23   2012017534

Manufactured in the United States of America
1 – BP – 12/31/12

CHAPTER ONE

"I just bought the cutest bathing suit," Morgan said in her third call to me that afternoon. "It's a bikini. And it's *tiny*. Billy's eyes are going to pop when he sees it."

While Morgan was out shopping, I was lying on the couch at my father's place, reviewing the Camp Spirit leadership manual. Morgan and I had been hired as counselors at the all-girls camp. We were due to leave in a few days.

"Billy is working in the city all summer," I reminded her. "He won't see you in your cute, tiny bikini."

"Yes, he will," Morgan said. "I'm going to try it on for him as soon as I get home."

"Good idea," I said. "Every guy wants to see his girl-friend in a bikini that she's going to be wearing around a bunch of other guys." There was a boys' camp across the lake from Camp Spirit. The counselors at both camps hung out together in their spare time.

"I *told* Billy to apply for a job at that boys' camp," Morgan said. "He was the one who decided to stay in the city all summer. What do you expect me to do, Robyn? Wear an old-lady bathing suit just because Billy didn't listen to good advice when he heard it?"

Before I could reply, I heard a blood-curdling scream.

"What was that?" I said into my phone. "Morgan, are you all right?"

I heard a thud. Then more screaming. Then a lot of voices all at once. Someone said something about an ambulance. Someone else said something about 9-1-1. Then all I heard was dead air.

I dialed Morgan's number. It rang a couple of times before kicking me into her voice mail. I tried again. No answer.

"Problem?" my dad said. He had come out of his study, coffee cup in hand, and was padding across the floor of his loft on his way to the kitchen for a refill.

"I was just talking to Morgan. I heard a scream and then . . ." I held out my phone.

"Was she in a car? On a bike?"

"She was at the mall."

"Well, I'm sure she's fine," my dad said. "As long as her credit card doesn't get refused, I don't think there's much trouble even Morgan can get into at the mall."

It turned out that my father was wrong.

. . .

"Broken," Morgan said when she called me again nearly three hours later. "And not a hairline fracture. It's spectacularly broken. I can't put any weight on it for at least six weeks, maybe longer."

"Six weeks? What about our jobs?"

"It's your job now," Morgan said. "I can't run around after a bunch of nine-year-olds if I'm on crutches."

"But—"

"I gotta go, Robyn. I want to give Billy the good news."

"Good news?"

"I'm going to be in the city all summer. I'll be able to see him every night. I'll call you later, okay?"

"Okay," I muttered. I sank down onto the couch.

"Problem?" my dad said again. He was coming out of the kitchen, coffee cup in hand—his third trip since I'd arrived—and heading back to his office. He was catching up on his paperwork.

"There was a freak accident at the mall. They have these giant beach balls hanging from the ceiling—part of their summer display. The cable holding one of them snapped, and the ball fell."

"Not on Morgan, I hope," my dad said, concerned now.

"No. It just fell. Turns out that the balls aren't heavy. But I guess most of the people at the mall didn't know that. Someone saw the ball falling and screamed. Then a whole bunch of other people panicked, and there was a stampede." At least, that's how Morgan had described it. "Morgan was on the stairs, heading down to a shoe store, and she got pushed. She broke her ankle. She'll be on crutches all summer."

"Ouch," my dad said.

"I only applied for the camp job because Morgan talked me into it. I don't know any of the other counselors."

"You'll make friends, Robbie. You always do."

I knew my dad was right. But it wouldn't be the same without Morgan.

"Where's Morgan now?" he said.

"She's on her way home."

My dad dug a set of keys out of his pocket and tossed them to me.

"Let's take a run over there," he said. "You can drive."

I stared at the keys. "You're going to let me drive your car?"

My dad has a Porsche. He is very particular about it. I had started taking driving lessons the minute I turned sixteen. My dad had been happy to go out for practice drives with me. But he had always borrowed our family friend Henri's car, which she hardly ever drove. Two weeks ago I had passed my second road test. I was now qualified to drive solo. My mom had let me borrow her car a couple of times to go to the mall. But my dad's Porsche?

My dad just shrugged. "Why not?" he said. "It's going to come to that sooner or later."

. . .

It turned out that Morgan's elation following her accident had a lot to do with the painkillers she had been given at the hospital. Once they wore off, her mood changed dramatically. By the next day she had turned into a major grouch. It didn't help that the day she broke her ankle was the same day Billy had chosen to surprise her. He had accepted a job as a counselor at—you guessed it—the boys' camp across the lake from Camp Spirit.

"I told him to tell them he'd changed his mind," Morgan said. "But he wouldn't do it. He said he'd signed a contract. Like that's some kind of big deal."

"Well, actually, it is," I said. My mom is a lawyer. True, she's a criminal lawyer. But while she was in law school, she suffered—as she put it—through contract law with the rest of her class. Now she always reads the fine print.

"You sound just like Billy," Morgan said, pouting. "It's fine for you. You'll be able to see him. In fact, you're going to keep an eye on him for me. I mean it. I'm not going to have some sun-bleached Camp Spirit counselor steal my boyfriend while I'm stuck here hobbling around this stupid city. Have you ever tried to get up and down stairs on crutches, Robyn? I'll be lucky if I don't break my other ankle."

She complained for another hour before I finally stood up.

"Where are you going?" she said.

"I . . . um . . . Nick and I are getting together—I only have a couple more days before I have to leave for camp."

Morgan perked up. "Right," she said. "Nick's going to be here all summer, and you're going to be there. Maybe he and I can hang out. Life's never dull around Nick. Hey, I'll keep an eye on him for you—you know, return the favor."

"That's an idea," I said. But not a very good one. Nick didn't out-and-out dislike Morgan. But he didn't have much in common with her, either. He also thought she was a little too self-absorbed, and he didn't understand why she and I were such good friends.

·   ·   ·

I found Nick in the park across the street from the used-to-be carpet factory that my dad owned. He'd had it transformed into living space for himself and added half a dozen apartments that brought him some nice rental income. Nick lived in one of those apartments.

Nick wasn't alone in the park. He was with a spiky-haired girl named Beej (short for B.J., which was short for something else that she refused to tell me) and an enormous black dog named Orion.

". . . twice a day, minimum," I heard Nick say as I darted through traffic to join him. He smiled when he saw me and slipped an arm around me.

Beej rolled her eyes.

"What are you doing?" I said to Nick.

"Giving Beej the short course."

"The short course on what?"

"The care and feeding of Orion," Beej said. "As if I've never looked after him before. I know what to do, Nick. It's not exactly rocket science."

"How come Beej is looking after Orion?" I said. "Are you going somewhere?"

"Yeah," Nick said. "It just came up. I was going to tell you."

I didn't like the sound of that. Nick had disappeared once before. He'd taken off without telling me—or anyone else, except for Beej—where he was going. I waited for an explanation.

"You're leaving in a couple of days for the whole summer," he said. "School's finished. I need a break. I thought I'd go up north for a while."

"Up north where?"

"We thought we'd do some hiking, some camping."

"We?"

"Me and a guy I know."

"What guy?"

"I thought leashes were for dogs," Beej said to Nick. "Does she always quiz you like this?"

I glowered at her.

"Just a guy," he said. "You don't know him. I met him at the group home."

All the guys Nick had met at the group home had been in trouble with the law.

"Don't give me that look, Robyn," he said. "He's an okay guy. He's not into anything."

"Except camping," I said. "Since when do you ever go camping?"

"Just because you've never seen me pitch a tent, doesn't mean I don't know how," Nick said. "I've been camping before."

"How long are you going to be gone?"

Beej shook her head. Nick ignored her.

"I don't know how long," he said. "We're gonna see how it goes. If we can find jobs, we might be away until fall. Come on, Robyn. I didn't give you a hard time when you told me you were going to be working at that camp all summer."

"I applied for that job ages ago," I said. "Before you and I got back together. And anyway, I thought you'd be able to come up on visiting days."

"I don't want to spend the whole summer in the city alone, Robyn."

"Will I be able to get in touch with you?"

"Not while I'm camping," Nick said. He didn't have a cell phone. "But whenever we get near a phone, I'll call. I promise."

"I won't always be able to answer," I said.

"I'll keep trying until I get you."

"When are you leaving?"

"Tomorrow."

"Tomorrow? When were you planning to tell me?"

"As soon as I finished telling Beej everything she

needs to know." He pulled me closer and kissed me on the cheek.

"Beej already knows everything she needs to know, especially now that Beej has this," Beej said, holding up several sheets of paper covered with Nick's handwriting. "Beej is getting out of here. No offense, but you guys are too much." She handed Orion's leash back to Nick. "I'll pick him up in the morning." She gave the dog a final scratch behind the ear, then took off.

"I'm going to miss you," I said, happy that I could snuggle up against him without Beej making faces.

"I'm going to miss you, too," Nick said.

I stayed at my dad's place that night so that I could go with Nick to the bus station the next morning. He was taking the bus north to where he would meet up with his friend. I eyed the large duffle bag he was carrying.

"You sure you have everything you need?"

"Yup."

"Sleeping bag?"

"In here." He patted the duffle bag. "And your dad lent me a pup tent."

"Where is it?"

"In here." When I looked skeptical, he added, "It folds down to nothing. And I'm an excellent packer."

We hugged in the bus bay, breathing in bus fumes, and Nick promised to call me the first chance he got. He held me until the bus driver announced "All aboard" for the third time. Then he found a seat by the window and waved at me until the bus was out of sight. He was right.

I was going to be away anyway. And if anyone deserved a little fun, it was Nick. He worked hard. He had to. He lived on his own. He had to work full-time while he went to school. He was always on the go, always had too many things to do. A couple of weeks out of town would do him good. And if he could find a job up there and make some money, even better.

.   .   .

"I miss Nick already," I said the next morning when I went into my father's kitchen to see what there was for breakfast.

My dad glanced up from the newspaper he had been reading.

"You know how I sometimes say that timing is everything?" he said.

"Yeah." I hunted around the fridge until I found a container of yogurt.

"Well, it really is, Robbie."

I perched on a stool beside my dad. "What are you talking about, Dad?"

"First Morgan breaks her ankle and can't go to camp, and the same day Billy announces that he's taken a camp job and now he's going to be away all summer while Morgan is stuck here in town."

I frowned. "First?" That didn't sound good.

My dad turned the newspaper around so that I could get a good look at the page he was reading—and at the picture on the page.

"Is that what I think it is?" I said.

"'Fraid so, Robbie."

I stared at the picture, scanned the article beside it, and groaned. Camp Spirit had burned to the ground the previous night, the fire blamed on a lightning strike. Now I was stuck in the city all summer too—without Nick.

My dad's buzzer sounded.

"I'll get it," I said. I went to the door, pressed the button on the wall beside it, and said hello.

"It's Beej," a voice said. "It says on Nick's list that I'm supposed to give Orion some special vitamins three times a week, but Nick forgot to give them to me."

"Didn't he give you a key to his place?"

"Do you think I'd be talking to you now if he had?"

I pictured her doing her too-familiar eye-roll.

"Meet me on the second floor," I said. I buzzed her in through the main-floor door.

My dad was already hooking a key off a key ring that hung in his kitchen. He had copies of the keys for each of the apartments on the second floor.

I went downstairs and opened Nick's door for Beej. She rummaged through his kitchen cupboards until she found what she was looking for. It was only when she was on her way back to the door that she noticed what I was staring at.

"I thought he went camping," she said, a puzzled expression on her face.

"That's what he said."

"So how come he left his sleeping bag and his tent here?"

The same question was flashing in my mind. So were a couple of others, like, what was in the bag he'd loaded onto the bus? If he wasn't going camping, where was he going?

Why had he lied to me—again?

CHAPTER **TWO**

"It's probably not what you think," Morgan said when I called her.

"You mean, he probably wasn't lying to me when he said he was going camping, even though he left his camping equipment behind in his apartment?"

"You don't have to bite my head off, Robyn. I'm just trying to make you feel better."

"Nick lied to me. He lied to my dad. I have no idea where he is. I can't contact him. I have no idea what he's even up to. What could you possibly say to make me feel better?"

"Maybe he forgot his stuff," Morgan said.

"Right."

Her voice brightened. "Hey, I know something that might cheer you up."

"Unless it involves getting hold of Nick this second and getting an explanation—"

"It involves you and me relaxing on the Point for the summer."

She meant the point of land that jutted out into an enormous sapphire-blue lake. The Point on which, way back when, Morgan's grandparents had built a summerhouse. Morgan had spent most of her summers on the Point. I'd spent a lot of time there too.

"I can't," I said. "I have to get a job."

"You don't have to," Morgan said. "It's not like you need the money. Your parents both have great jobs. You could take one more summer off. Come on, Robyn. I'm gonna go crazy if I have to stay in the city all summer, and my parents won't let me go up north by myself, especially with a broken ankle. Besides, it wouldn't be any fun if I was up there all by my lonesome. But if you came with me . . . Please?"

"I'm going to be seventeen soon," I said. "And I've never had a real job."

"So?"

"So, it's time."

The truth was, I felt self-conscious about the fact that I didn't have to worry about money, while Nick had to work every spare minute to keep a roof over his head. He didn't have a phone. I did. He had to budget to be able to afford a new pair of jeans. I had a clothing allowance. When we went to the movies or for coffee and I offered to treat, he usually looked embarrassed. But he let me sometimes because he couldn't always afford to pay.

"I have to find a job, Morgan. If you don't go up north, we can hang out together in the evenings and on weekends."

. . .

My phone trilled the next day. I checked the display, hoping to see *Unknown name*. It would mean that Nick was calling me. Instead, I saw a name—Anthony Turner. Morgan's father.

"Robyn, hello," Dr. Turner boomed. "Morgan told me about your little problem."

Little problem? What had Morgan said?

"I think I might be able to help you out," he said. "If you're interested, that is."

"Um, interested in what, Dr. Turner?"

"A job. Morgan said you were determined to find a job this summer. And now that that camp has burned down . . . I know quite a few people up north. I've spent more summers up there than I can remember. Even worked up there a few summers myself. So—I hope you don't mind—when Morgan explained your predicament, I made a few phone calls."

"You didn't have to do that," I said. "I've got a lot of feelers out." The day before, I had sent out résumés to more than a dozen different places. I had also visited every mall in the area to fill out applications. But so far . . .

"As a matter of fact, I did," he said with a laugh. "You know Morgan. She can be persistent. I spoke with an old friend on your behalf. He publishes a couple of community newspapers up in cabin country. He had a student lined up to work for him this summer, but at the last minute the kid apparently got a better offer. I mentioned that I know a bright young woman who's in the market for summer employment. He's looking for someone who can write up ads, send invoices, do proofreading, things like that. It's pretty basic office stuff, Robyn, strictly entry-level. But if you're interested, he'd like to talk to you."

"Really?"

"Got a pencil handy?"

I scrambled for one and wrote down the name and number he gave me. "He's a great guy, and he'll be expecting your call."

I could have hugged him.

"Thanks, Dr. Turner."

"All I did was mention your name. Check it out. See what you think. Doug's a great guy."

. . .

I got the job!

My dad congratulated me. Dr. Turner said he knew I was a shoo-in. My mom's fiancé, Ted, said he was thrilled for me. Morgan squealed with delight. My mother said, "No."

"What do you mean, no?" I'd said. "I already said I'd take the job."

"Well, now you're going to have to say that you can't," my mom had said, which was why my dad and I were on our way to her house together to discuss the matter.

Ted answered the doorbell.

"How's the packing going?" I asked him.

He and my mom were about to leave for a month-long vacation.

"I'm all set," he said. "But I think your mother's preparations are going to go down to the wire." If I knew my mom, she was packing and repacking her suitcase. She tended to pack on a you-never-know basis. In other words, she packed a lot of things just in case she might need them, then took them out again because maybe she wouldn't need them after all, and then repacked them because, well, you never know.

He opened the door wide to let us in. Sure enough, we found my mom in front of a suitcase that lay open on the dining room table, surrounded by stacks of neatly folded clothes. She was staring at them in exasperation but smiled when I entered the room. Her smile faded as soon as she saw my father.

"Mac, what are you doing here?" she said.

"Patti." My father grinned at her. "You look marvelous."

My mom shot me a disapproving look. The rule, since my parents had separated and ultimately divorced, was that my dad was allowed in my mom's house only if she personally invited him, which she never did.

"I asked Dad to come," I said. "About my job . . ."

"I thought we already agreed that you weren't going to take that job," my mom said.

"You agreed. But I don't understand what the problem is. I want this job, Mom. And they want me. Mr. Griffith said I was the perfect candidate."

Sensing a fight, Ted started to back out of the room.

"Oh no you don't." My mom glowered at him. "I know you've been encouraging her."

"I congratulated her," Ted said. "It'll be a wonderful experience for her."

"No, it won't," my mom said. "She's not going."

"Hey, have you two set the date yet?" my dad said, clearly enjoying himself. He wasn't at all fazed when my mother scowled at him. In fact, she and Ted hadn't set the wedding date yet. Ted was hoping that the vacation would relax my mom so that they could finally discuss concrete plans.

"Please, Mom," I said. "I really want this job."

"No."

"Why not?"

"It's too far away."

"It's in the town where Morgan's summerhouse is. I've been there a million times." Okay, slight exaggeration. But I had spent a couple of weeks there several times.

"That's different. You were always with Morgan and her parents."

"They're going to come up on weekends," I said. Well, maybe on a few weekends. "And Morgan's dad knows the paper's publisher and the editor."

"Didn't you say this job requires you to drive?"

"Yes, but—"

"You only just got your license."

"She's a good driver, Patti," my father said. "She drove over here."

My mother stared at him in astonishment. "You let her drive your car?"

He nodded. "And she handled it like a pro."

"She *is* a good driver," Ted said. He had taken me practice driving almost every day before my second road test.

My mom shot him a furious look.

"Besides," Ted said, "Robyn will be on side roads where the traffic is light, not on highways. All the kids up there drive at Robyn's age, Patricia. I was driving at that age. It's the only way to get around."

My dad regarded Ted with what looked like grudging respect.

"She doesn't have a car," my mom said.

"She does if she wants it," Ted said, smiling at me. "A buddy of mine has an old clunker that he's trying to get rid of." He caught the look in my mom's eyes. "It's road-ready and perfectly safe," Ted assured her. "It's yours if you want it, Robyn. My contribution to the employment effort."

"But she's only sixteen," my mother said.

"She'll be seventeen in a couple of months, Patti," my dad said.

"I'll be out of the country. What if something goes wrong?"

"I'm here," my dad said. "And if she needs anyone closer, she can always contact Dean Lafayette. He's still up there. Still chief of police. Robbie can always go to him if anything happens."

My dad and Dean Lafayette had gone through the academy together. Every time I went to Morgan's place up north, my dad made me promise to say hi, but I hardly ever did.

"I can call him and let him know she'll be up there," he said.

In fact, he already had called. But, wisely, he didn't tell my mom that.

"Please, Mom? I already said yes. And Morgan and I have it all worked out."

We had come up with what we thought was an excellent plan. We would live together at Morgan's summerhouse. Morgan would amuse herself during the day while I worked, and we would spend evenings and weekends hanging out together. Morgan's parents had agreed to it. My dad didn't have a problem with it. Ted liked the idea. Still, it took forever before my mom finally said, "I don't know . . ." which, for her, was progress.

"Come on, Patti," my dad said. "She's not a baby anymore. You want her to be independent, don't you?"

My mom's eyes misted over. She bit her lip.

"You have to promise that you'll call your father regularly while Ted and I are away," she said.

"No problem."

"And you have to promise that you and Morgan will lock up every night—doors and windows, Robyn."

"Done."

"And no boys in the house after dark."

My dad and Ted looked at each other. They were probably thinking the same thing that I was—anything that Morgan and I could possibly do with boys in the dark, we could just as easily do when it was light.

"Sure, Mom. So is it okay? Can I go?"

"Well . . ."

I held my breath. My mother glanced at my father, then at Ted, who nodded at her.

"Okay," she said.

I hugged her.

"I was just about to start dinner, Mac," Ted said. "Would you like to stay?"

My mom looked daggers at Ted.

"Thanks," my dad said graciously. "But I thought I'd take Robbie out to celebrate. You two have a good trip, Patti." He kissed my mom on the lips before she could protest. She scowled at him. Ted smiled benignly.

.   .   .

"Something wrong with your food, Robbie?" my dad said. We were sitting in my dad's usual booth at La Folie. My dad was making good progress with his order of fish. I was picking at my vegetarian curry.

"No, it's fine," I said.

"Are you worried about how you're going to do on the job?"

"Something like that," I said. But I wasn't. Really, I was worried about Nick. I still hadn't heard from him. But I didn't tell my dad that. I didn't want him to know that Nick had lied to me and that he had disappeared again.

"You'll be fine," my dad said. "There'll be a learning curve. There always is. But I know you, Robbie. You'll catch on. Before you know it you'll be bored to tears."

Which, of course, wasn't at all what happened.

CHAPTER **THREE**

"You're not going to be like this all summer, are you?" Morgan said.

"Huh?" I said.

"You're sulking about Nick, aren't you?" she said.

"No, I'm not." I was focusing one hundred percent on the road ahead of me. This was the first time that I had driven without an adult in the car with me. It took a lot of concentration.

"Yes, you are. You haven't said a word in almost an hour. I get it, Robyn. I really do. But you've got to let it go. Otherwise you're going to ruin the summer for both of us." She nudged me gently. "You said things were going okay with you two."

"They were," I said without taking my eyes off the road. "At least, I thought they were." Now I wasn't so sure.

"Then relax," Morgan said. "He said he would call.

And he will. Then you can find out what's going on. In the meantime, try to focus on the positives. This is going to be great. Well, as great as anything can be on crutches. We're going to have the whole house to ourselves. We can tan naked on the dock if we want to."

Why would I want to do that? I wondered.

"You've got a job," she went on. "And we've got a car."

We did indeed. Just before Ted and my mother had left for the airport, Ted had dropped a set of keys into my hand. "Are these what I think they are?" I'd asked.

Ted had touched a finger to his lips. "Your mother still doesn't approve. The less she hears about it, the better." I couldn't help smiling. Ted is small and balding and kind of nerdy-looking; he's a wildly successful financial analyst too. He's also quiet, modest, and unassuming, and he loves jazz—in other words, he's the complete opposite of my tall, flashy, super confident ex-cop rock-and-roll-loving father. But when it comes to handling my mother, the two of them have a lot in common. I wondered if my mom had realized it yet. "It's just an old beater, but it will get you through the summer." He handed me an envelope. "Registration and insurance," he said. I had thrown my arms around him and hugged him.

"Of course, it's not much of a car," Morgan said as we drove north. "It's kind of . . . old."

"I told you it was." It was a ten-year-old Toyota.

"I know. But I didn't think it would be this old. I thought Ted was loaded."

"It's just for the summer, Morgan."

"I know. But it's not exactly a boy magnet . . ."

"What about Billy?"

Morgan rolled her eyes. "It's going to be a long summer, Robyn. We have to have some fun."

"I guess," I said, staring out the windshield.

Morgan sighed. "A very long summer."

. . .

It was late afternoon by the time I pulled into the parking lot of the town's only grocery store. I hopped out, circled the Toyota, and opened Morgan's door for her.

"Come on," I said. "We have to get groceries."

"My ankle hurts. I'll wait for you here."

"Oh no you don't. If I do the shopping, you'll spend the rest of the week complaining that I bought all the wrong things."

"But it's late," she complained.

"All the more reason to get moving. Come on. We'll shop, drive to the marina, load up the boat, and get out to the Point." Morgan's summerhouse was surrounded by water on three sides and by forest on the fourth. There was no road directly to it. Morgan's family got to and from the house by boat. "We can eat on the deck and watch the sunset."

Morgan grumbled, but she struggled out of the car and into the grocery store, where we shopped. Well, where I shopped. Morgan hobbled along behind me, alternately whining about her crutches and checking out every guy she saw between the ages of sixteen and twenty-six, which consisted of one acne-suffering shelf stocker, one gangly guy trailing down the aisles with a woman who could only have been his mother, and—

"Wow," Morgan gasped.

I turned to see what was wow-worthy and found her gaping at a tall, sandy-haired guy in jeans and a T-shirt that did nothing to hide what looked like some impressive biceps. He was pushing an overflowing cart up to the cashier.

"Billy, Billy, Billy," I whispered in Morgan's ear. "Besides," I added, "he looks like he's at least twenty."

"I'm just looking," she said. Actually, she was staring. And drooling. It was a good thing she was on crutches. They were all that kept her upright when, twenty minutes later, as I was struggling to hoist an enormous jug of water out of the bottom of the supermarket cart, the guy appeared out of nowhere and asked, "Need some help with that?"

"Uh, sure," I said. I stepped aside. He scooped up the jug as if it were no heavier than a single water bottle and slid it into the Toyota's backseat for me. "Thanks," I said.

"No problem."

He went back to where he had come from, a black pickup truck, and a moment later was pulling out onto the main street.

"Oh my god, he's amazing. And built. Did you see—"

"Get in the car, Morgan."

We drove down to the marina where Morgan's parents keep a motorboat. I looked around as I unloaded our suitcases and the groceries from the car. The lake was a shimmering blue. The woods around it were a deep green, dotted here and there with summerhouses, each with a beachfront and a dock. The marina itself consisted of multiple docks for motorboats and sailboats. Directly across from the marina was the local police station.

"I should go over and say hi to Chief Lafayette," I said.

Morgan groaned. "Can't it wait until tomorrow? My ankle is killing me. I just want to get out to the Point and relax."

We did what Morgan wanted. She sat on the dock while I carried our stuff from the car to the boat. After I loaded everything, I had to help Morgan into the boat, which was harder than it probably sounds. She was super protective of her broken ankle and not good at balancing on one foot. She put all her weight on me as she struggled into the boat. She was still clutching my arm when she dropped down onto a seat, throwing me off balance. I had to scramble to stop myself from ending up in the water.

We put on our life jackets, and I cast off. Morgan, who has been boating back and forth to the Point ever since she was a toddler, took us across the lake.

As soon as we had finished unpacking and I had put all the groceries away, Morgan declared that she was hungry. We decided what we wanted to eat, and then, of course, I had to make it. Turns out it's very difficult to cook when you're tottering around on crutches. It's also difficult to set the table, clear the table, and wash the dishes afterwards. Morgan was right—it was going to be a long summer.

After dinner we sat out on the veranda and watched the sun set.

"This is my favorite time of day," Morgan said. "It gets so quiet when the sun goes down." The only thing we could hear was the call of the loons somewhere out on the water. Morgan sighed with contentment. "So, when do you have to be at work?"

"Nine o'clock. You sure you're going to be okay here all alone, Morgan? What if you have an emergency?"

"I have a phone. So do you."

"But I'll have the boat."

"I'll be fine," Morgan assured me. "If anything happens, I'll call you. If I can't get you, I'll call Mr. Duggan at the marina. And if I can't get him, I'll call the cops. But, really, what could happen? Most summers, my biggest problem is boredom."

I looked out over the peaceful lake and decided she was right. Really, what could happen?

.　.　.

The next morning I made sandwiches for both of us and left Morgan's in the fridge for her. Morgan hobbled down to the dock to give me a crash course on how to operate the boat.

"Maybe you should take me over," I said as I listened to her instructions for the second time and watched her demonstrate yet again what I was supposed to do. "Then you can bring the boat back and pick me up after work."

"I can't get in and out of the boat by myself," she reminded me. "Besides, operating a boat is a lot easier than driving a car, Robyn. Just go slowly, that's all. Come on, I'll walk you through the start-up again."

I followed her instructions and made it across the lake to the marina, but I panicked when I saw how fast the dock was rushing up to meet me. When I tried to throttle back the engine, it died on me, and I couldn't get it started again.

"You've flooded it," someone called out. A girl standing on the dock. She picked up a rope. "Catch." I grabbed it, and she pulled me toward the dock. "Haven't been in boats much, huh?" she said.

"Not alone," I confessed.

She helped me tie up and then jumped into the boat and showed me how to get the engine going and how to slow it down again without flooding it.

"You sure know your way around," I said.

She laughed. "I grew up around boats. My dad owns the marina."

"Mr. Duggan?"

"That's right." She sounded surprised.

"I'm staying with my friend Morgan," I said. "Over there." I pointed to where I had just come from.

"Sure. I know her. Well, I know who she is. She comes up here every summer with her parents. I saw you arrive yesterday. What happened to her leg?"

"Broke her ankle."

"Are you two up here on vacation?"

"Morgan is. I have a job. At the *Lakesider*. I'm Robyn."

"Colleen."

We chatted for a few minutes, then I asked her for directions to the newspaper office. My stomach was alive with butterflies as I steered the Toyota out of the marina parking lot and headed into town. Turns out I could have walked from the marina. Car safely parked, I drew in a deep breath and pushed open the front door of the low-rise brick building that housed the *Lakesider News*. I approached a woman inside and asked to see Mr. Griffith, the publisher.

"Doug, someone's here to see you," she called across the room.

A tall man with a shock of steel-grey hair looked up from the doorway to a private office. He strode over to where I was standing, grasped my hand, and shook it enthusiastically.

"Robyn. Great to meet you in person," he said. "Tony had a lot of good things to say about you." He meant Morgan's dad. "Are you all settled in?"

"Yes, thank you."

"Excellent. Well, come on. Let me show you around."

He introduced me to the rest of the staff—Gloria Zorros, who handled the paper's advertising; Rob

Hartford, editor and features reporter; Tom Matheson, the paper's sole full-time general reporter; and Nan Sullivan, who copyedited all of the paper's content, proofed everything, coordinated distribution, and took care of office supplies—"among other things," Mr. Griffith said.

"You'll be working with just about everyone, Robyn. Summer is our busiest time of the year. With all the tourists up here, all the summer events, we carry a lot of ads and have a lot more news to cover. I'll leave you with Gloria this morning. She can answer any questions you have. But you're going to have to be flexible, Robyn. Are you okay with that?"

I assured him I was.

I spent the morning with Gloria, who showed me how to take down requests for classified ads. She also showed me everything I needed to know about what she called "display advertising"—any ad that wasn't a classified ad. "You can give them the prices, the deadlines, and the sizes," she said. "If they have any other questions, pass them on to me." She showed me the computer system and gave me a user name and a password. By lunchtime my head was spinning. That's when Rob Hartford called me into his office.

"I have an important job for you, Robyn," he said. "You think you're up for it?"

"I guess so," I said. But I was having a hard enough time remembering everything that Gloria had spent the morning showing me.

Mr. Hartford opened a desk drawer and pulled out a reporter's notebook and a ballpoint pen. He handed them to me.

"Two blocks down, on the other side of the street, there's an establishment called Roxy's," he said solemnly. "Your assignment"—assignment!—"is to take everyone's lunch order, collect their money, and bring back lunch." When I just stood there thinking, he nodded at the notebook in my hand. Well, Dr. Turner had said there would probably be a lot of gofer work. I scribbled down Mr. Hartford's lunch order.

Twenty minutes later, armed with my order pad, er, reporter's notebook, I headed down to Roxy's. I was on my way back holding a cardboard box filled with sandwiches, salads, and beverages, when a kid burst out of a record store right in front of me and bolted into the street.

"Oh no you don't!" a red-faced man yelled. He darted out of the store and grabbed the kid by the collar of his T-shirt. The kid struggled, but the man kept an iron grip on him. "I'm holding you for the police, you brat," he said.

"He didn't do nothing," someone said. Another kid grabbed the first kid by the arm. "Come on, Lucas. Let's get out of here."

"He's not going anywhere until he hands over the DVDs he took," the man said.

"Let me go," the first kid said. But he didn't struggle very hard. The man had him firmly by the collar, and a crowd had started to gather.

"You think I'm blind?" the man said. "Or maybe you think I'm stupid. I watched you take those DVDs. The police are on their way."

As if on cue, a police cruiser rolled up at the curb and an officer got out. He was a big man whose eyes were hidden behind mirrored sunglasses. Despite the heat of the day, he was wearing a long-sleeved shirt and gloves. He had on the same sturdy boots that my dad used to wear when he was a patrol officer.

"What seems to be the problem?" he said.

"These kids were shoplifting, that's what," the storeowner said, still holding the struggling kid.

"He didn't do nothin'," the second kid said again.

The crowd had swelled even more once the police arrived. I looked down at the lunch order I was carrying. *I should probably get it back to the office*, I thought—but what if this turned out to be news?

The police officer told the kid to step over to the cruiser and empty his pockets onto the hood of the car.

The kid glanced at his friend, who shook his head in defeat. Then he pulled a wad of tissues and a battered pack of gum from one of the side pockets of his jeans and a handful of small change from the other. The officer started patting the kid down and paused as he ran his hand down the kid's back.

"What's that?" he said.

The kid just shrugged.

"Take it out and put it on the car," the officer said.

Someone pushed past me through the crowd.

"What's going on here, Officer?" he said. He was a burly man with salt-and-pepper hair and a soft voice. He was wearing a short-sleeved shirt tucked into a pair of loose-fitting jeans. "That's one of my kids."

"I'm aware of that, Mr. Wilson," the officer said. He never took his eyes off the kid. "Go on," he said. "Put it on the car."

The kid hung his head as he reached around and pulled two DVDs from the back of his pants.

"See?" the storeowner said. "What did I tell you? Thief. I want him arrested."

Another police cruiser pulled up, and a second officer got out. This one was older than the first one and wore a short-sleeved uniform shirt. He was also wearing sunglasses, but he took them off when he got out of the car. Dean Lafayette, my father's old friend.

"What seems to be the problem, Phil?" he said to the first officer.

"That kid was stealing from my store, that's what," the storeowner said.

The first police officer, Phil, nodded to the DVDs that were sitting on the hood of the car.

"We can give him a warning, George," Dean Lafayette said.

"I found stolen goods on him, Chief," Phil said.

"There you go," the storeowner said triumphantly.

"Come on, George," Lafayette said. "Phil is new on the job. He's still learning how we do things around here. This is just a boy. You've got your merchandise back. What do you say we get the kid to agree he won't set foot in your store again and leave it at that?"

"Warning?" the storeowner said. "You've got to be kidding! Last time I checked, stealing was a criminal offense. I want him arrested."

"Chief, may I say something?" Mr. Wilson said.

Lafayette nodded.

"Lucas has been with me for less than a month," Wilson continued. "If you arrest him, he's going to end up back in a juvenile detention facility."

"Which is exactly where he belongs," the storeowner said.

"It's where they all belong," said a man standing next to me.

Wilson shook his head. He appealed again to the chief of police. "You know what those places are like. Sending him back there isn't going to help him. Give him a warning. Release him to me. I'll see to it that he stays on my property and that he does extra chores. He'll learn more from that then he ever would from being locked up again. Please. He's just a kid, and not a bad one, either, despite what you might think."

Dean Lafayette seemed to consider this for a few moments. He turned to the storeowner.

"What do you say, George?"

The storeowner shook his head. "Those kids are nothing but trouble."

"Just one chance, that's all I'm asking," Wilson said.

"If he messes up again, you can throw the book at him."

Lafayette looked at the storeowner again. The man was glowering at the kid he'd caught stealing. I was pretty sure he was going to press charges.

"One chance," Mr. Wilson said again. "You name the conditions, and I'll see that he abides by them."

"It's up to you, George," the chief said.

"Fine," the storeowner grumbled. "He doesn't set foot in my store again. *None* of your kids do."

"That's not fair," the second kid wailed. "I didn't do anything."

"And I want that one searched, too," the storeowner said.

"But I didn't do anything," the kid said again.

Wilson nodded his agreement. Phil gestured to the second kid to step over to the patrol car and empty his pockets. He patted him down but didn't find any stolen goods.

"See?" the kid said. "I didn't touch your stupid stuff."

"That's enough, Tal," Mr. Wilson said. He looked at Lafayette. "So, are we good here, Chief?"

The chief turned to the storeowner. The storeowner gave a curt nod.

"Lucas, apologize to the man," Mr. Wilson said.

Lucas scooped up the loose change that he had taken from his pocket and deposited on the roof of the police car. He jammed it in his pocket.

"Apologize now, Lucas," Mr. Wilson said, "before I change my mind and let the chief throw the book at you."

"Sorry," Lucas muttered under his breath.

The storeowner stared at him with disgust. "If one of your kids ever comes into my store again, he's going to be sorry, Wilson."

"You'd better get these boys back to your place, Larry," Lafayette said to Wilson. Then he turned to the crowd. "Okay, folks. We're all done here."

As the crowd dispersed, I heard people muttering about those kids. "Nothing but trouble," one person said. "Just like the government to take all these delinquents and send them up to a peaceful town like this where they make nothing but trouble," someone else added.

The chief spoke to the other officer for a moment before starting back to his cruiser. I intercepted him.

"Excuse me," I said. "My dad said I should say hi."

"Robyn! Good Lord, you're all grown-up. Seems to me that the last time I spotted you around town, you were all arms and legs."

"It's been a couple of years," I said. I'd spent all of the previous summer in the city. The summer before that, Morgan had been away.

"Well, it's good to see you. Mac told me you were coming up here." He fished in his pocket for a business card, pulled out a pen, and scribbled a phone number on the back of it. "Here's where you can reach me. And that's my cell-phone number on the back. If you need anything, anything at all, just give me a call."

I thanked him.

"What was that all about?" I said, tucking his card

into a pocket. "Who were those kids?"

"Just a couple of Larry's kids. Larry Wilson runs a group home for teens who have been in trouble with the law. He puts them to work, teaches them a trade, helps them get their lives back on track."

"It sounds like not everyone appreciates what he's doing," I said.

Lafayette shrugged. "This is a small town. We get a lot of summer people up here. Some of them have been coming up for generations. But the people who live here year-round don't consider them part of the community. They feel the same way about Larry's kids, even though they only come into town about once a week, if that. A lot of the locals see them as troublemakers."

"Are they?"

"They can be a little rough around the edges—and cocky when they first arrive at Larry's. But Larry mostly keeps them in line. Even manages to teach them some manners. That said, I wouldn't recommend them as appropriate company. Your dad would probably have my head if he thought I'd expose you to boys like that."

I wondered what Chief Lafayette would think if he met Nick.

"Enjoy your summer, Robyn," he said. "Call anytime. And check with the ranger station if you decide to do any hiking in the area. We've had a few incidents involving bears."

"Bears?"

"There seem to be more of them around this year.

From what we can tell, they're hungry, and a few of them are acting a little bolder than we'd like. A couple of people have had bad scares. The rangers are tracking them as best they can. They can tell you what areas to avoid and what precautions to take."

"It's okay," I said. "I wasn't planning to do a lot of hiking." Not with Morgan on crutches. And certainly not after what I had just heard.

When I got back to the office with everyone's lunches there was a truck out front. A man was throwing down bundles of newspapers.

"Hot off the press," Doug Griffith said.

I glanced at the photo on the front page. It was a medium shot of a big brown bear out in the woods somewhere. The headline above it read "Bear Crisis."

. . .

"Hold on a minute, Billy," Morgan said that night after dark. She watched as I did a circuit of the summerhouse's main floor. "What are you doing, Robyn?"

"Checking the windows."

Morgan shook her head. "You really need to relax. In all the years I've been coming up here, I've only ever seen bears out at the garbage dump."

"You saw the headline," I said. "I'm not taking any chances." I looked more closely at the phone she was holding. "Hey, is that mine?"

"Sorry. I forgot to recharge mine after last night."

She meant, after she had talked to Billy for nearly two hours. I didn't begrudge her such a loyal boyfriend, but her gabfest reminded me that I still hadn't heard from Nick. "And I promised Billy—" She suddenly remembered that he was still on the line. "Sorry, Billy," she said into my phone.

"Don't forget to recharge your phone when you're finished," I said. "And while you're at it, recharge mine."

She nodded, her way of telling me not to worry.

CHAPTER **FOUR**

At noon the next day, Mr. Hartford waved me into his office again. I grabbed a notebook and a pen and took them with me.

"I've got an assignment for you, Robyn," he said.

I flipped to a clean page in my notebook and waited for him to give me his lunch order.

"Tom's up in Eden interviewing a bear-attack victim—"

"There was a bear attack?"

"The man he's interviewing was attacked by a bear five years ago—while he was hiking in the mountains out west. Tom's doing a story about how he survived the attack, a couple sidebars on proper precautions and what to do if you run into a bear. We get a lot of tourists up here who wander off into the woods like they're strolling through a city park. The *Lakesider* has a role to play in making sure they use a little common sense. In my experience, there's nothing like a good bear-attack story to make folks sit up and listen.

"I've got to go down to Westly," he continued. "The politicos are making an announcement about funding a new hospital for the area. So I was wondering how you'd feel about handling a story—bit of a fluff piece, but a good photo op. You know how to operate a camera, right?"

"Sure."

"Great. There's a new camp opening this afternoon. For kids with cancer. It's funded by a foundation set up by that movie star—the one who started that organic snack company and donated all the profits to charity. His wife's here for the grand opening. All I want you to do is drive out there with a camera and a pocket recorder, take a few pictures, talk to a couple of the kids and their parents, see if you can get a quote from the wife—she was pretty big herself for a while—and bring it all back here. Tom or Nan can write it up if you don't feel comfortable doing it. Or you can take a first run at it if you'd like. What do you say?"

"Well, I—"

"Doug told me that English is one of your best subjects at school. Think of it as a school assignment—and you get to meet a movie star."

A used-to-be movie star whose movies I had never seen. But still . . .

"Okay, sure," I said. How hard could it be?

Hartford gave me a map and marked my route on it

with a yellow highlighter.

"It's a little out of the way," he said. "And most of the driving is on dirt roads, which will slow you down a little. Give yourself at least an hour to get there."

I shoved the map, the camera, and the audio recorder into my tote bag and hurried down to the marina parking lot. I rummaged around in the bag for my keys. Not there. I checked my pocket. No keys. Where were they?

I ransacked my bag again, then emptied it onto the hood of my car. Still no keys. I glanced through the driver's side window—and there they were, on the floor! I had driven across town after work the day before to pick up a bunch of things that Morgan had insisted she needed—sunscreen, a special moisturizer, some organic snacks that she had acquired a taste for, thanks to Billy. But I'd been distracted—I'd been thinking about Nick—and must have dropped my keys.

I checked my watch. If I didn't get going, I'd be late for my first-ever reporting assignment.

I tried the driver's-side door. It was locked. I tried the other three doors. Locked, locked, and locked. *Okay,* I thought, *what to do?*

Coat hanger—people in movies tackled situations like this with a coat hanger. I ran to the marina restaurant to see if I could borrow a wire hanger.

And all their hangers were plastic.

"Problem?" said a quiet voice behind me.

I spun around and found myself face-to-face with the police officer who had responded to the call at the record store. I couldn't see his eyes behind his mirrored sunglasses.

"I locked my keys in my car," I said, "and I'm late for an assignment. I'm working at the paper for the summer."

"I can give you a hand with that. Where's your car?"

I led him to the parking lot. He walked around my car, inspecting it closely. Then he walked over to a police cruiser that was parked nearby. He opened the trunk and hunted inside. He returned carrying a thin piece of metal.

"What's that?" I asked.

"It's called a slim jim. Just the thing for opening locked doors." He fed the thin strip of metal between the top of the driver's side window and the doorframe, worked it down inside, and—yes!—popped the lock.

"Thank you!" I could have hugged him. Well, maybe not. But it would have been terrible if I'd missed the camp opening.

"No problem," he said. "Part of the job. For some reason, summer people are always locking their keys in their cars." His voice echoed with disapproval. "Drive safely."

I got into my car, checked the map Mr. Hartford had given me, and drove out of the lot. Once I got to the camp, I shoved the map and my keys into my bag and grabbed the pocket recorder and camera off the front seat. I'd arrived just in time to take the grand tour. After that I met some of the kids and their parents, took some pictures, and listened to speeches by the movie star's wife, the camp director, some local politicians, and a couple of the kids who would be attending the camp's first two-week session. The speeches were followed by a corn roast, which I opted to skip. I got in my car and headed back to town.

At least, I thought I was heading back to town. I drove down the dirt path that led to the gravel road and made a turn. I had the windows down—the air conditioner in Ted's friend's old Toyota seemed to be on the fritz—and was feeling pleased with myself for having handled the assignment so well. The movie star's wife had answered all of my questions—and then thanked me for coming. She'd even given me an autographed photo of her husband for Ted, who was a huge fan.

Thirty minutes later I came to an unfamiliar cross-road. Almost every intersection that I had passed that day had had posts with signs pointing the way to camps and summer homes. I hadn't paid much attention to them. But there was a pole at this intersection with a huge spruce tree–shaped sign advertising a cut-your-own Christmas tree business. I didn't remember seeing it on the way to the camp. I drove on for another ten minutes, watching for anything that looked remotely familiar. Disoriented, I pulled over to the side of the road to check my map.

Big problem.

I was sure I had put the map into my bag, but it wasn't there. I turned the bag upside down, dumping the contents onto the seat. The map was definitely gone. I had set my bag down during the speeches so that I could take some pictures. One of those big floppy satchels that's open at the top. You could cram a lot of stuff into it, but there was nothing to stop things from falling out if you dropped it. I scrabbled through the bag again.

No map.

It had been nearly forty-five minutes since I'd left the camp. If I had been going in the right direction, I would have been getting close to town. I would have passed the occasional house. But I hadn't. I was still driving past dense forest on either side of the road and, every ten miles or so, a dirt crossroad leading to summer homes located along even smaller, narrower dirt roads.

So obviously I was going in the wrong direction. All I had to do was turn around and head back the way I had come.

I executed a three-point turn that would have made my father proud and started back toward the camp. Easy, right?

So why, as the sun began to dip toward the tree line, didn't I pass the camp? *It's probably just a little farther*, I told myself every few minutes.

The sun disappeared behind the trees. When it gets dark out in the country, it really gets dark. There were no streetlights, no lights from nearby houses. Nothing except a half-moon overhead that gave off just enough light to cast weird shadows in the deep woods on either side of the road. A creepy-crawly feeling crept down my spine. I glanced at the Toyota's gas gauge. I had a quarter tank left. That would be enough to get me back to town, right? Assuming I could find town.

But what if I couldn't?

Totally confused and increasingly panicky, I groped in my bag for my phone. I would call Morgan. Or maybe Dean Lafayette. Or Doug Griffith. I would do my best to describe where I was. Then I would sit tight and wait for someone to come and get me.

Something darted across the road. Something big—bigish. A deer?

I swerved to avoid hitting it.

And went off the road into the ditch.

My seat belt mostly did its job, but my head slammed against the steering wheel. It took me a few moments—maybe longer—to absorb what had happened. I raised a hand to my throbbing forehead. I wasn't bleeding, so that was good, but I felt a lump forming. I would probably end up with an ugly bruise. And now I wasn't just lost. I was in a ditch, and I wasn't sure that I was going to be able to get out.

I felt over the passenger seat for my phone. It wasn't there. It must have fallen when I swerved to avoid whatever it was that had run across the road. I unbuckled my seat belt and ran my hand over the floor.

Found it.

I moved my thumb across the touch screen. Nothing.

The battery was dead. Morgan had used it to talk to Billy for hours last night. She must have forgotten to recharge it when she had finished. There was nothing I could do about that.

I put the car in reverse and stepped on the gas to back out of the ditch.

No luck.

I tried again. The car's wheels spun, but the car didn't move. I told myself not to panic. I told myself that if I didn't get back to the house, Morgan would eventually call the newspaper—assuming it was still open. If it wasn't . . . Morgan is smart. She would call the police. Chief Lafayette would know how to contact Mr. Hartford, who would tell him about my assignment. Someone would come looking for me. Or maybe a car would pass—except that I hadn't seen another car since I had left the camp.

Morgan would do something when I didn't show up at the Point. She would call someone. Everything would be okay.

I stayed calm for the first half hour.

Then I caught a glimpse of something out in the woods to my right. Something big and lumbering. My heart pounded. I rolled up all the windows and squinted into the darkness. I wished I had a flashlight. Then I remembered who had arranged for the car. Mr. Thinks-of-Everything—Ted. Maybe there was a light in the trunk. I peered into the darkness again. Whatever I had seen was gone. Had it wandered away? Or was it lying in wait behind a tree or a rock, ready to attack?

Cautiously, I opened the driver's-side door. I circled

around to the trunk, unlocked it, and groped inside. Jack. Tire iron. Something long and tubular. Yes! A flashlight. I turned it on and pointed it into the woods—right into a pair of eyes set into a smallish head attached to a large brown body.

I ran back to the driver's-side door, got into the car, and locked all the doors. I sat there, heart racing, afraid to look out again and just as afraid not to. I tried to think of what I knew about bears. It wasn't much. Did they ever attack people in cars? Could a bear break a car window? Could a bear—

Light flashed in my side-view mirror.

I twisted around in my seat and saw headlights in the distance behind me. They grew brighter. I reached for the door handle and then hesitated. What about the bear?

But I had to do something.

I pushed the door open and stepped up out of the ditch just as a pickup truck roared past me. I turned on the flashlight and shone it at the back of the truck. Too late. It disappeared around a bend.

I felt like crying. Then I remembered the bear.

I dashed back to the car, got inside, and locked the door.

I was going to kill Morgan—assuming I survived the night.

I was going to—

Two red lights got brighter and brighter from around the bend where the truck had just disappeared.

It took me a moment to realize that they were taillights. The truck was backing up. I turned on the flashlight and waved it so that the driver could see me in the ditch.

The truck came to a stop alongside me.

Saved, I thought.

Both cab doors opened, and two men got out.

That's when it occurred to me I might be in even greater danger now—I was alone in the dark in the middle of nowhere. No one had any idea where I was. And two strange men were coming toward me.

The creepy-crawly feeling overtook me again.

CHAPTER **FIVE**

One of the men circled around to the passenger side of my car. The other one approached the driver's side. I gasped as his face appeared in the window beside me. He rapped on the window and gestured for me to roll it down. I did. Just a crack.

"You okay?" he said.

I stared up at him. It was the same guy Morgan and I had seen in the grocery store on our first day in town, the guy who had put the jug of bottled water in my car for me.

"Are you hurt?" he said.

"I got lost. Then a deer or something ran across the road. I swerved and—" It was only fair to warn him. "I saw a bear over there." I pointed.

"Why don't you get out of there and sit in the truck while Derek and I take a look at your car?" he said.

I hesitated.

He peered in at me.

"If I had a phone with me, I'd call someone for you," he said. "But I don't. Look, I know how you probably feel. You're a girl, you're all alone out here, we're two strange guys—I'm Bruno, by the way. If you want, we'll leave. When we get where we're going, we'll call someone for you and let them know where you are. You want us to do that?"

I nodded.

"Okay. Just sit tight."

He straightened up and called to Derek. The two of them headed back to their truck and got in. I heard the engine turn over and saw the headlights go on.

"Wait!" I called, getting out of the car. "Wait!" I ran to the driver's side of the truck. Bruno rolled down his window.

"I recognize you from the grocery store on Sunday," I said.

He flashed me a smile.

"I recognize you, too," he said. "But that's no guarantee, right?"

"Guarantee?"

"That I'm not some crazy serial killer who's trying to lure you into my truck." His smile widened. Morgan was right. He was cute.

"Do you live near here?" I asked.

"Ten minutes up the road and east at the next turn."

I heard voices in my head—my mother's and my father's. My mom was telling me, "Do not—do you hear me, Robyn?—do not ever get into a pickup truck with two strangers." My dad—miracle of miracles—was actually agreeing with her. But neither of them had seen that bear.

"Just let me get my bag," I said.

I ran back to the car—and I do mean ran—dug a piece of paper and a pen out of my bag, and scrawled a note: I have gone with Bruno and Derek. Black pickup truck. I included the make and license number. I put the note in the glove compartment, locked the car, and ran back to the truck. Derek had gotten out so that I could slide in between him and Bruno. We drove the first few minutes in silence.

"You a townie?" Bruno said at last.

"I have a job up here for the summer. You?"

"I'm here year-round. We both are."

As we turned a corner, I saw lights up ahead on the left. My whole body tensed up. He hadn't lied about how close he was to home. But what did home look like? And what would happen once I got there?

A few minutes later the truck turned off the road. Bruno tooted the horn as he approached a gate set into a high chain-link fence. I felt myself tense up again when the gate slid shut behind us.

We were in a compound of some kind. A large stone house stood far back from the road. I saw the shadowy expanses of other buildings in the compound, but most of them were dark. What kind of place was this? Bruno steered the truck toward the one building that had lights

on. It was a large, squat structure that held several cars—
a garage. I recognized one of the guys standing around
the cars and breathed a sigh of relief. Larry Wilson. He
came out of the building to meet the truck.

"We picked up a damsel in distress," Bruno said. He
jumped down from the truck and reached up to help me
out. "Her car went in a ditch."

"Larry Wilson," Mr. Wilson said to me, thrusting
out a hand.

"Robyn Hunter," I said.

We shook hands.

"Are you hurt?" Wilson said.

"I banged my head, but otherwise I'm fine."

"Well, come into the light. Let me take a look."

When I stepped into the building, half a dozen
boys—most of them looked younger than Bruno and
Derek—straightened up and stared at me. I spotted
Lucas, the kid who had stolen the DVDs, and the friend
who had tried to defend him.

"You're going to have a nasty bump," Wilson said
after he inspected my forehead. "You should probably
get that checked out when you get home." He turned to
Bruno. "What shape is her car in?"

"Couldn't see any serious damage," Derek said. "But
we'll have to tow it out of the ditch . . ."

"Do you have your car keys with you, or did you
leave them in the car?" Mr. Wilson asked me.

"I have them."

"If you give them to Bruno and Derek, they'll take

the tow truck, get your car out of the ditch. Then we can see if there's any damage. If it's good to go, you can be on your way. If it isn't, I'll give you a lift home. Or you can call your folks and ask them to come get you."

I fished my keys out of my bag and handed them to Bruno. He and Derek walked across the yard and got into a tow truck.

"Do you have a phone I can use?" I asked.

"Up at the house," Wilson said. "In the kitchen. The front door is open."

I followed the long gravel driveway up to the house and let myself in. The house was tidy and comfortably furnished. It was also eerily silent. I guessed that all of Larry's kids were down in the garage with him. I went through to an enormous, spotless kitchen with a phone mounted on the wall and dialed Morgan's number.

"Hello?" she said. There was a faraway quality to her voice.

"It's me," I said.

"Robyn?" She sounded confused. "What time is it?"

I had woken her up. I suddenly realized how lucky I was that Bruno and Derek had happened along. If I had counted on Morgan for help, I would have been in that ditch all night.

"It's late," I said, glancing at my watch.

"Where are you?" Morgan said. "What are you doing?"

"I'm in the middle of nowhere. My car is in a ditch. I had a close encounter with a bear. You didn't even notice that I was missing, did you?"

"A bear?" Morgan said. "Ohmygod, are you okay?"

"I'm fine. I'm at Larry Wilson's place."

"Who's Larry Wilson?"

"Write down the name. And write down this phone number, too."

"Wait a sec." I heard a bump, bump, bump at the other end of the line and pictured Morgan hopping across the room in search of a pen. She sounded breathless when she finally said, "Okay. Ready." I read Wilson's phone number to her. "I'll call you if they can't fix my car. Okay?"

"Okay. But you're not hurt? You're safe?"

"So far. I'll see you later, okay?" At least, I hoped I would.

I hung up the phone and started back down the driveway to the garage. Started, but suddenly stopped when someone grabbed me from behind, clapped a hand over my mouth, and dragged me behind a dark building.

I kicked. I struggled. I tried to bite. Then I felt hot breath against my ear, and a voice whispered, "Don't scream. I'm not going to hurt you."

My whole body went limp.

CHAPTER SIX

I felt his breath in my ear.

"If I take my hand away from your mouth, promise you won't scream? Promise you'll keep your voice down?"

I nodded.

I felt his hand relax and finally fall away from my mouth. I turned slowly. A sliver of moonlight fell across his face, illuminating a pair of purple-blue eyes and a jagged scar that ran from the bridge of his nose to the base of his right ear.

"What are you doing here, Robyn?" he said.

"What am I doing here? What are you doing here? I thought you went camping."

Nick glanced around, as if he were afraid someone might see us. He pulled me deeper into the shadows.

"Seriously, Robyn, why are you here?"

"The camp where I was supposed to work burned

down. I had to get another job. I'm staying with Morgan. What's going on, Nick?"

"I can't explain it to you now. You have to trust me."

"But—"

"Just, whatever happens, you don't know me, okay?"

"What?"

"You'd better get back."

"But—"

"I'll be in touch. I'll explain. I promise."

He shoved me gently but firmly toward the gravel driveway. I fought the urge to look over my shoulder as I walked back to the garage. But my mind raced. What was going on? What was Nick doing at Larry Wilson's place? Why had he lied about where he was going? And why did he want me to pretend that I didn't know him?

"Is everything okay?" Wilson said when I stepped into the garage again. "Did you get hold of your parents?"

"A friend," I said. "I'm up here with my friend for the summer."

Someone shuffled into the building. Nick. I glanced at him but tried not to register any emotion on my face. A few moments later, the tow truck pulled up in front of the garage and Bruno jumped out.

"You have a couple of dents that maybe you didn't have before," he said. "But other than that, your car's fine."

My blue Toyota pulled up behind the tow truck and Derek got out. "You could stand a tune-up," he said as he tossed me my keys.

Mr. Wilson walked slowly around my car, pausing to inspect the body.

"The boys can fix those dings for you if you want," he said. "Give you a tune-up, too, no charge."

"Thanks," I said. "But it's late, and it's been a long day."

"Well, another time, then," Wilson said. He fished in his pocket for a business card and handed it to me. "If you want my guys to take a look at it, give me a call."

One of the boys watching shook his head and muttered something under his breath. Tal, the kid who had defended the shoplifter.

"Do you have something to say, Tal?" Wilson asked him. "Why don't you say it louder so we can all hear it?"

"It was nothing," Tal muttered.

Mr. Wilson glanced at the kid standing next to Tal, who shifted his gaze down at the ground. Wilson's eyes went back to Tal.

"We're waiting, Tal."

Tal met Wilson's eyes. "I said, 'I bet she won't let us touch her car.' I bet no one in town would. They don't trust us.'"

"Thank you, Tal," Wilson said. "That wasn't so difficult, was it?" He turned back to me. "The offer stands. Some of these boys are better than any mechanic you'll find in town."

Tal looked at me with sullen eyes, and I thought about what had happened outside the record store. I also thought about how some people regarded Nick, purely based on his background.

"Thank you for the offer, Mr. Wilson," I said. "I'll call you when I have time to bring my car back. And I appreciate what you did for me tonight."

"No problem," he said.

I turned to go to my car but found Bruno blocking my path. He handed me a piece of paper. There was a small map sketched on it and a set of directions printed neatly below.

"So you don't get lost again on your way back to town," he said.

I thanked him. It was only after I had gotten in the car and started the engine that I realized there was something written on the other side of the paper. I turned it over. My cheeks burned as I glanced out the window and saw Bruno looking at me. He was grinning. He had written the directions on the back of the note I had left in the glove compartment.

. . .

"You have nothing to be embarrassed about," Morgan said. "For all you knew, he could have been an axe-murderer."

The directions that Bruno had given me turned out to be excellent. I made it back to town without a hitch, parked in the marina parking lot, and boated across the water under the moon. I'd found Morgan waiting anxiously for me on the dock. We'd retreated to the veranda, where I told her what had happened.

"Yeah, but he wasn't an axe-murderer," I said. "He's nice. The guys out there are all like Nick. They've been in trouble, but they're getting their acts together."

"What about Nick?" Morgan said. "What's he doing there?"

"I have no idea." All I knew was that he hadn't trusted me enough to tell me the truth.

"Well, look on the bright side," Morgan said. "At least you know where he is."

Somehow, that didn't help.

. . .

The next day Gloria kept me busy making invoices for all the people who had placed classifieds in the paper. It was late afternoon before I had a chance to tackle the story about the camp opening. By the time I was on my third and hopefully final draft, there was only one other person still in the office—Tom Matheson. He was talking on the phone and working on his computer at the same time. When he hung up, he shut down his computer, leaned back in his chair, and looked across the room at me.

"How's the story coming?" he said. "Want me to take a look at it for you?" Before I could answer, he'd propelled his wheeled chair across the room to where I was working. I scooched aside so that he could take a look. "Hmmm," he said as he read. I couldn't tell if that was good or bad. He nudged me gently aside and started to type. "There," he said ten minutes later, pushing his chair away from the desk. "I didn't change much—just punched it up a little." He grinned at me.

I skimmed the revised story. It read much better.

"Thanks, Tom."

Tom was the oldest person on staff—he was in his late sixties—but he'd insisted right from the start that I call him by his first name. Mr. Hartford had told me that Tom had been a reporter at a major daily newspaper for most of his life. He had been laid off ten years ago and had moved up here, supposedly to retire and take it easy. At least that's what Tom had promised his wife. "But he has ink in his veins. Tom's wife, Lucy, asked me to hire him part-time so that he wouldn't drive her crazy moping around the house. Part-time somehow turned into full-time. Lucy usually has to call him to remind him to get home for dinner."

"It's a good article, Robyn," Tom said to me. "All the facts, a little human interest—the quotes from those kids and their parents are terrific. Are you considering a career in journalism?"

"Me?"

"You sound surprised."

"It's just that I'd never thought about it."

"For what it's worth, I think you'd be good at it." He shot himself back to his own desk and stood up.

"Can I ask you something, Tom?"

"Shoot."

"It's about Mr. Wilson."

"Larry?"

"You know him?"

"I've interviewed him a few times. More than a few. He generates a fair bit of controversy around here. He and those kids of his."

"A lot of people don't seem to like them."

Tom shrugged. "Part of it's a NIMBY thing. Most people would agree that kids like that—kids who have been in trouble—need some help turning their lives around. In principle. But given a choice in the matter, they all tend to say the same thing—Not In My Back Yard. Part of that's 'cause of the kids themselves. They're not exactly angels. Some of them have gotten into trouble up here. A couple instances of recreational drug use, one kid got pinched for a couple of B and Es . . . then there's the issue of the local girls."

"What about them?"

"Apparently some of Larry's kids are considered hot commodities—so I've been told. They've generated a lot of anxiety on the part of parents who don't relish the thought of their darling daughters taking up with juvenile delinquents—their term, not mine. It's been more than two years now since Larry started his group home, and there's still a sizable group of people lobbying to shut him down and get the kids shipped back to where they came from."

"Do you think that will happen?"

Tom shrugged. "From what I've seen, Larry rides those kids hard. He's fair, but he's tough on them. If they get in trouble, he sees to it that they make restitution. If all else fails, they know they could get shipped back to a detention facility in the city—"

The phone rang. Tom reached for it and for a pen at the same time.

"*Lakesider*," he said, his hand poised over a reporter's notebook. "Is it? Already?" He thrust out a hand to check his watch. "I must have lost track of the time. No, no, don't throw it out. I'll be walking through the door in five minutes." He hung up and reached for the hat that covered his balding head outdoors. "The wife is threatening to pitch my dinner into the garbage. Gotta run. Lock up, will you, Robyn?"

I was just finishing up when I heard footsteps coming down a flight of stairs. A side door to the office opened and a head peeked in.

"Oh, I was hoping someone was still here," said a cheery voice. "I'm Margie Harris. I'm with the local historical society upstairs. Actually, I am the historical society." She was a plump woman with close-cropped grey hair. "I was just preparing a grant proposal, and my printer ran out of paper. Doug usually doesn't mind if I borrow a few sheets."

"Help yourself," I said.

She smiled absently at me, collected some paper from a cupboard near the stairs, and shuffled back upstairs. I printed out my article and left it on Mr. Hartford's desk.

.   .   .

It took me forever to fall asleep that night. I kept thinking about Nick and wondering when he was going to get in touch with me. I envied Morgan. Billy called her every night after his campers were tucked into their cabins, and they talked for ages. Morgan always looked relaxed when she was on the phone with him. She didn't have to worry about what he was doing or if he was okay—ever. I, on the other hand . . .

I know that I finally drifted off to sleep because I almost had a heart attack when someone grabbed me and shook me awake.

"Robyn," a voice hissed.

"Jeez, Morgan, you scared me. What are you—"

She shushed me. "I think I heard something. Outside."

"Define something."

"A noise. And rattling. You don't think it's a bear, do you?"

"You said bears never come around here," I reminded her.

"There's a first time for everything. What if . . ."

After a thump somewhere downstairs, we both stiffened.

"Ohmygod," Morgan whimpered. "What if it is a bear?"

"You saw me check the doors and windows before we came upstairs," I said. "They're all closed. And locked."

Morgan whimpered again. "I was hot. I went outside for some air before I came upstairs. I don't know if I locked the door again."

"Terrific."

The stairs creaked.

"It's coming up here," Morgan said. Her face looked silvery white in the moonlight that was streaming through my window. "Where's your phone?"

I had left it on my bedside table. I fumbled for it in the darkness—and accidentally knocked it onto the bare wood floor. It landed with a clunk.

We both froze.

For a moment we heard nothing.

Then something banged against the door to my room. Morgan screamed.

"Robyn?" an alarmed-sounding voice said. "Robyn, are you okay?"

It was Nick.

CHAPTER **SEVEN**

Nick was standing in the door to my room, wearing nothing but a surfer-style bathing suit. His black hair was plastered to his head, and he was dripping water all over the floor.

"You scared us to death," I said. My heart was still hammering in my chest, but I was glad to see him. I untangled myself from Morgan, who had thrown herself at me in terror.

"I need to talk to you, Robyn," Nick said. "I don't have much time." His teeth were chattering.

"You need to dry off." I ran down the hall to the bathroom and brought him back some big bath towels. He wrapped one around his waist and used the other one to dry his hair and torso. As he toweled off, I saw Morgan staring at two nasty scars on his back. Nick caught her doing it and immediately draped the towel over his shoulders.

"I heard about your ankle," he said, nodding at the cast on Morgan's foot. "I know what that's like." Nick had broken his ankle last fall.

"Nick, what's going on?" I said.

Nick glanced self-consciously at Morgan. I was pretty sure he didn't want to talk in front of her. I nodded at the door.

"Oh no you don't," Morgan said. "This is my house. You scared me, Nick. If you're going to tell Robyn what's going on, you'll have to tell me, too, because I'm not leaving."

Nick looked pleadingly at me, but it didn't do any good. Next to Nick, Morgan is the most stubborn person I know. All I could do was shrug.

"I didn't mean to wake you," he said to Morgan. "And I'm sorry I scared you." He turned to me. "Is it okay if I sit down?"

I nodded.

He pulled a chair from the corner of the room. I perched on the edge of the bed.

"What are you doing up here, Nick? And why didn't you tell me where you were going?"

"I thought if I told you, you'd try to stop me." I'd heard that before, usually about the same time I found out how much trouble Nick was in.

"So you decided to lie to me instead?"

"I'm sorry, Robyn. I really am." He glanced at Morgan again, but there was no way she was going to leave. "You were going to be out of town all summer anyway. I thought I could just take care of things and be back before you and everything would be fine."

"Take care of what things?" I said.

"I promised to do something for this guy I know."

The guys Nick knew tended to be guys who had been in trouble.

"What guy? Do what?"

I was expecting him to be evasive—Nick wasn't always direct with me—but he surprised me by answering right away.

"His name is Seth Richmond. I've known him my whole life. His mom and my mom were friends. He lived on our street before my mom married Duane." Duane was Nick's stepfather. He was the one who'd given Nick the scar on his face. He was also responsible for Nick being an orphan. "He's about ten years older than me. He's been looking after his brother, Alex, since their mom died in a work accident. Alex was a year younger than me, but we used to hang out. About the same time as my mom hooked up with Duane, Seth was diagnosed with Hodgkin's lymphoma. It's a kind of cancer."

"I thought it had a pretty good recovery rate," Morgan said. Morgan knew a lot about medical stuff on account of her parents. Her mom is a psychiatrist. Her dad is a surgeon.

"Maybe," Nick said. "I didn't study up on it or anything. All I know is that Seth got really sick. He couldn't look after Alex anymore. So Alex got sent into foster care. It didn't work out. Alex didn't like his foster parents—any of them. He'd always get into trouble, and then he'd run away.

"Seth was really worried about what was going to happen to Alex if he . . . you know. He started checking into options for Alex besides foster care. Someone told him about this guy up here who runs a group home and who trains kids to be mechanics."

"Larry Wilson," I said.

Nick nodded. "It sounded good. So Seth arranged for Alex to come up here. Things seemed to go okay for a while. Seth said Alex liked working with cars. He seemed to get along okay with Larry and the other kids. Then, out of the blue, Seth got a call from Alex—Alex didn't want to be at the home anymore, he wanted to go back to the city. But he wouldn't tell Seth why. He just said that he didn't like it and that he couldn't explain it over the phone. Seth told him to give it a little more time."

Nick paused and let out a long sigh. "Seth's cancer has spread. They've given him all kinds of treatments. Some of them have made him feel even worse. They told him he has maybe six months to live. Seth told Larry that. He was trying to arrange for a visit with Alex—he wanted to tell Alex in person. He was waiting for Larry to call him back."

"And he didn't?" I said.

"Larry called, all right. But it wasn't about the visit. He had bad news for Seth."

"What kind of bad news?"

"That Alex was dead."

"Poor Seth," I said.

"Poor Alex," Nick said.

"What happened to him?"

"Suicide. At least, that was the coroner's ruling. The police up here did an investigation—guys at Larry's who knew Alex said that he'd become really quiet."

"Maybe he was worried about his brother," I said.

"That's what I thought," Nick said. "But Seth doesn't believe it."

"You just said that he told you Alex wasn't happy up here."

"That's what Alex told Seth," Nick said. "But Seth says Alex wasn't the kind of person to kill himself just because he was unhappy where he was. He'd be more likely to just take off, the way he did when he was in foster care. He always went back to Seth, even when Seth was in the hospital."

"But if the guys at Mr. Wilson's place said he got quiet, maybe he was depressed—"

"That's what I told Seth," Nick said. "But he's Alex's brother. He talked to Alex on the phone. He said Alex didn't sound depressed. He said he sounded unhappy, but that there's a difference between that and depression, and he's pretty sure he knows which is which. He tried to push the coroner to do some kind of inquiry. But no one up here saw any reason for it."

"What does he think happened?" Morgan asked.

"I don't think he thinks anything in particular. But

the guys there . . . maybe Alex got into some kind of beef with one of them. Or maybe . . ." He shook his head. "It could have been an accident, but Seth doubts it because Alex was a good swimmer. The thing is, Seth is going to die. Before he does, he wants to know for sure what happened to Alex. If Alex really drowned himself, okay, he says he's gonna have to accept that. It's really eating at him. He thinks he failed Alex."

"It's not his fault he got sick," I said.

"I know. He probably does too. But that doesn't stop him from wishing there was something else he could have done. He asked me to come up here and see what I could find out."

"Does Mr. Wilson know why you're there? Does he know you knew Alex?"

Nick shook his head. "All he knows is that I saw a notice about his place at a youth center. Larry's Place. I called the number on it and talked to Larry Wilson. The next time he came to town, we got together. He explained his program to me. I asked him if I could be part of it. At first I thought he was going to say no. He asked me if I had a probation officer or something. I didn't want to get my social worker involved, so I said I didn't anymore, that I was living on my own and I wanted to make some changes. Maybe learn a trade. He finally agreed to take me."

"And?" Morgan said, her eyes glistening with excitement. "What have you found out?"

He shrugged. "Not much. Larry told me when I

arrived that if anything was bothering me, I should tell him. He said some guys keep things bottled up and that's not good—that they only make their problems worse. I don't know if he meant Alex, but I got the feeling he did."

"What about the other guys out there? What did they say about Alex?" I said.

"I haven't talked to them about him yet. The guys who are there, they've been around, you know? They don't open up fast. You have to earn their trust before they'll talk to you. But I have to tell you, I've been here a week now and I really like the place. Some of the guys are kind of messed up, and Larry's strict. You screw up and he makes you deal with it. But he's fair, and he's a whole lot nicer than some of the social workers I've met. Plus I'm learning a lot about cars. Larry says I have a real aptitude. He asked me if I know anything about computers."

"Computers?"

"Cars have a lot of computerized parts now," Morgan said. "It's getting so you practically have to be Steve Jobs to work in an auto plant."

"Larry says cars are getting more complicated to fix," Nick continued. "Mechanics have to know all about that stuff now, but that if I work hard, I could maybe consider getting into something like that. It'd be a good living. He said I should think about taking some computer courses."

"Do the guys out there go to school?"

"I talked to one guy who's been taking courses on-line. I think a couple of other guys are doing that too. But none of them go to an actual school. Not now, anyway. Larry says he hopes some of them will get their GEDs, but that right now most of them have other issues to deal with." He glanced at the clock on my bedside table. "I should get going. I know some guys sneak out some-times—some of them have had things going with local girls. But I also heard that if Larry catches you it's extra chores and no town privileges for a month."

"How did you get here?" I asked. "Larry's place is half an hour from town."

"I hitched a ride," he said. "I hope I can hitch one back. If not . . ."

"I could drive you."

He shook his head. "If I get caught, that's one thing. But I don't want you involved. It could blow my cover."

"Do you want me to talk to the police for you, see if I can find out anything?"

"I don't want you to do a thing. Besides, Seth already talked to the cops. They've made up their minds."

"What about my dad? Maybe he can—"

Nick took my hands in his. "See, that's why I didn't want to tell you, Robyn. I figured you'd be off at camp and I could just poke around and see if I could find out anything for Seth."

"I just want to help."

"I know. But there's nothing you can do. I don't want to make a big deal out of this. Seth's a good guy.

I just want to see what I can find out, you know, so he doesn't . . . you do your job, Robyn, and let me do this for Seth."

"How long are you planning to stay there?"

He shook his head. "I don't know. A couple weeks, I guess, until I get settled enough to start asking some questions or until I hear what guys are saying. Don't worry, I'll be fine. To be honest, I kind of like working on cars. Maybe I'll learn enough so that when I get back, I can buy myself an old beater and keep it running." He stood up and said goodbye to Morgan.

"I'll take you across in the boat," I said.

He shook his head. "Someone might see us. I don't want to take that chance. I haven't been out of the compound since I arrived, Robyn. It would be pretty hard to explain being seen in a boat with a girl, especially one who works at a newspaper. I'll go back the same way I got here. Besides, I stashed my clothes on the shore."

"At least let me walk down to the dock with you," I said.

When we got outside, he pulled me to him.

"I'm glad you're okay, Nick," I said, squirming away from him. "But you shouldn't have lied to me. When I saw your tent in your apartment—"

"You were in my apartment?"

I had to backtrack and tell him about Beej's surprise visit.

"I was mad at you," I added. "And worried. Really worried."

"I'm sorry." He tried to look suitably contrite. "It's just that—"

"Just that what?"

"I was kind of mad at you, too, going away for the whole summer."

I peered into his eyes. "You mean you were going to miss me?"

"Things are so busy during the school year. I guess I thought we'd have more time together."

I wrapped my arms around him, snuggled close, and tipped my head back so that he could kiss me. I didn't want to let him go. But after a few moments he eased himself free, and we walked hand-in-hand to the end of the dock.

"I wish I could stay," he said.

"Can you call me every once in a while, let me know you're okay?"

"I'll see what I can do." He sat on the edge of the dock, getting ready to slip into the water. I sat down beside him.

"Nick?" I said. "You don't think someone killed Alex, do you?"

Nick looked out over the water. "I don't know. I've been around a lot of guys like the ones at Mr. Wilson's place. I'm not saying it was premeditated murder or anything. But guys like that—they can do things without thinking. Maybe someone was giving Alex a hard time— or maybe Alex was giving someone a hard time. He could be like that, Robyn. Things can get out of control.

Believe me, I know. And in places like that, guys cover for other guys."

I squeezed his hand. I didn't know everything there was to know about Nick, but he had told me about some of what he had gone through—enough that I knew he was speaking from experience. "If there was something going on, if someone was responsible for what happened to Alex—directly or indirectly—I'm going to find out. It's the least I can do for Seth."

"Be careful, Nick. Don't do anything stupid. And if you find out anything—anything at all—promise me you'll go to the cops. The chief of police here is a friend of my dad's. He can—"

Nick pulled me to him and kissed me again. "I'll be careful, I promise." Then he eased himself into the water and swam off into the darkness. For a few minutes I followed his progress. Then a cloud slipped across the moon, and I lost him. By the time it reemerged from behind the clouds, Nick was gone. He could be so secretive and so frustrating. But whatever his shortcomings, he was a loyal friend. I didn't think there was anything Nick wouldn't do to help someone he cared about. I was just turning to go back up to the house when I saw something across the lake. Someone was standing on the dock at the marina. I couldn't make out who it was—it was too far and too dark. Well, if I couldn't see who it was, then that person couldn't see who I was or who Nick was—could they?

Morgan was still sitting on my bed when I went back inside.

"Wow," she said. "Nick looks amazing in a bathing suit. I didn't know he worked out, Robyn."

I had to admit he looked pretty good.

"But what's with those scars on his back? Was he in an accident?"

"A fight." Nick had told me all about it. "It was a bunch of guys against Nick. If a pizza delivery guy hadn't intervened . . . He was in the hospital for weeks, but it was a long time ago."

"No wonder he works out," Morgan said. "He looks like he can take care of himself now, if he has to."

I hoped he wouldn't have to.

CHAPTER **EIGHT**

The days seemed to drag by after Nick's visit. I was sitting at the end of the dock the following Monday night, trailing my bare feet in the water and watching the sun set, when my phone rang. I picked it up eagerly and checked the display, hoping maybe Nick had managed to get to a phone. But it was my father.

"Robbie," he boomed into my ear. "How are things in the fifth estate?"

"The what?"

"The press. How's it going?"

"I'm not exactly the press, Dad. I spent today at the beach, handing out free copies of the paper to tourists and summer people."

"Good for you. It's all about eyeballs, Robbie."

"If you say so. What's new with you, Dad?"

"That's why I'm calling. I have to go out of town for

a little while."

"How long?"

"A couple weeks."

"But you promised Mom—"

"How is she anyway?" my dad said. "Have you heard from her?"

"She's fine. She called from Paris." You wouldn't have known it by the conversation, though. All she wanted to talk about was road safety. "Dad, you promised her—"

"I know. Something came up. You'll still be able to get me by phone. I'll just be a few days away from you instead of a few hours."

"A few days? Where are you going?"

"Singapore."

"Singapore? What for?"

"Business. I'll be in a different time zone. Half the time I'll be in a different day. But you should be able to get hold of me anytime. If something comes up and you need someone right away, call Dean. Okay?"

I said okay. I considered telling him that I had run into Nick but decided against it. Nick wanted to do this on his own.

Morgan and her crutches thumped down to the end of the dock after I had hung up.

"Wanna watch a movie or something?" she said. Her summerhouse was equipped with a satellite dish. "We can make popcorn."

"Aren't you waiting for Billy to call?"

She shook her head. "He's on a canoe trip. I won't

be able to talk to him until the end of the week. So, how about it?"

"Okay." I looked down at the business card I was holding. "Just let me make a call."

"I'll go start the popcorn."

While Morgan made her way back up to the house, I flipped open my phone and keyed in the number on the business card.

"Mr. Wilson? This is Robyn Hunter. About that tune-up you offered me . . ."

.   .   .

"I might be a little late getting back after work," I told Morgan the next day. "You sure you don't want to run me across to the marina? That way you'll have the boat."

"I'll be fine," Morgan said. "I've still got a pile of magazines from yesterday." I had picked her up after work and taken her into town for some shopping. She had loaded up on magazines, which, of course, I had to carry for her. "What's up? Do you have to work late?"

"I'm getting the car tuned up. At Larry Wilson's place."

Morgan gave me a look. "Does Nick know?"

"Not yet."

"Didn't he tell you—"

"Now that I know where he is, it's torture not to be able to see him."

"But you're not supposed to know him."

"I'm not planning to talk to him. I'm just getting the car tuned up. That's all."

"Right," Morgan said. "That's all."

"Well, plus I'll be able to see for myself that he's okay. Nothing's going to happen."

.   .   .

As soon as I finished work, I drove out to Mr. Wilson's place. I stopped at the gate and pressed the buzzer attached to an intercom on the fence. The gate started to rumble open. I drove slowly up the gravel driveway to the garage. Mr. Wilson was working on a beat-up old car with two group-home residents. Bruno had a couple more with him. Nick wasn't in either group.

"Robyn, good to see you again," Wilson said. He wiped his hands on a rag as he came out to greet me. "Hey, guys, you remember Robyn."

Most of the boys looked away as soon as I smiled at them—except Bruno, who grinned and asked me if I was managing to stay out of ditches.

"So far, so good," I said. Morgan would have melted if she'd been there with me. He had his shirt off and was displaying his awesome six-pack. Even I couldn't help but admire the shape he was in.

"Give Bruno your keys," Mr. Wilson said. "He'll take care of your car. We'll go to the house to wait. The kitchen crew is working on dinner. I'm sure we can get someone to rustle us up some lemonade."

As we walked up to the house he pointed out the compound's garages, its classroom building, its bunkhouse. "The place started out as a car graveyard. I salvaged and fixed whatever I could. Still do. I trained as a mechanic in the armed forces. Then I spent some time teaching at a technical high school. That's what got me interested in what I'm doing now. I'd get these kids in my class—tough guys who were only there because they weren't old enough to drop out yet. They figured my class would be an easy credit. Well, they were wrong about that. I made them work—really work. Some of them couldn't hack it. They'd skip, just like they skipped the rest of their classes.

"The ones who stuck with it, though, started to change. They'd fix something and it would work, and it was like they couldn't believe it. Then they'd want to learn more. The kids had finally found something they could do, and that made them feel good.

"One thing led to another, and I left teaching and moved up here. But I'd read about some of the stuff that was happening down in the city, some of the trouble kids were getting themselves into. I started to wonder what would happen if I got some of those kids out into the country, laid down some rules, and taught them a trade. Maybe they'd end up with decent jobs instead of prison sentences."

We climbed the porch steps, and he held the door open for me. This time when I entered the house, it was full of life. Music was coming from speakers in the living room. Mr. Wilson immediately turned it down a few notches. A guy poked his head in, looking like he was ready to yell at whoever had messed with the volume. But when he saw it was Wilson, he quickly disappeared again. Mr. Wilson winked at me.

"Come on," he said.

He led me through to the spacious kitchen. Three guys in chef's aprons were preparing the evening meal. One was chopping vegetables for a salad. One was adding seasoning to a huge pot of something on the stove. The third, Lucas, who had been banned from the record store, was setting the kitchen's long table.

"Smells good, guys," Mr. Wilson said. "This is Robyn. We're giving her a tune-up. Lucas, how about getting us a couple of glasses of lemonade?" He turned to me. "We'll sit out on the back porch. It's nice and cool out there this time of day."

I followed him outside. That's when I finally spotted Nick. He and Derek, one of the guys who had rescued me from the ditch, had their shirts off and were chopping wood beside a lean-to that was half-full of firewood.

"I keep the boys busy," Wilson said. "But none of it is busywork. Come winter, that wood will help to keep the house warm. I've got fifty acres. In season, we even do a little hunting, get a deer or two. They make good meat."

Lucas appeared with two frosty glasses of lemonade on a tray. Mr. Wilson waved me into a chair. We sipped lemonade while he asked me about my job and my plans for the future. I glanced at Nick every now and then, but he never looked back at me. He was right about Wilson, though. He was no-nonsense but really nice. It seemed like no time at all before Bruno appeared and announced he'd finished with my car.

"Supper is almost ready," Wilson said. "You're welcome to stay, Robyn."

"Thanks," I said. "But I can't. I already made plans."

"Perhaps another time then." He stood up. "Bruno will show you to your car." He walked to the veranda railing. "Nick, Derek, time to wash up for supper."

Nick put down his axe and grabbed a T-shirt that was balled up on the ground. He used it to wipe the sweat from his face, neck, and torso. He glanced at me, but there was no recognition in his eyes.

"Come on," Bruno said. He led me around the house and back down to the garage.

"How long have you been here?" I asked him.

"Me? Eighteen months. Maybe a little longer."

"No offense, but aren't you kind of old for a group home?" I said. Except for Bruno, Derek, and Mr. Wilson, all the guys looked like they were Nick's age or younger.

"I help Larry," Bruno said. "And I teach the kids about cars."

"You like it?"

"Yeah. Larry's a good guy, not that anyone in town would ever believe it."

"They probably just don't know you guys well enough."

"They don't want to know us. But that's their problem, right?"

He stood beside my car as I started it and seemed pleased when I agreed that the engine seemed to be running more smoothly.

"Maybe I'll see you around," he said.

. . .

The next day, Mr. Hartford poked his head into the newspaper's cramped file room. "Looking for something?" he said.

I was seated at a small table with a stack of newspapers in front of me. It was my lunch break, and I was using the time to read through back issues of the *Lakesider*.

"Just curious," I said.

"About?"

"Larry Wilson and what he's doing for the kids who live with him."

He nodded.

"They've gotten a lot of coverage," I said.

I had started out looking for an article about Alex Richmond's death and had found it. It wasn't long. Alex's death was mentioned in the first paragraph. The rest of the article was about how Wilson's place was the subject of local controversy. I'd flipped through more issues of the paper and found articles that had been written when Wilson was just starting the place. Most of the articles consisted of coverage of town meetings at which residents protested the group home. They didn't want "a bunch of thugs" coming into town and causing trouble. But the smaller towns that were closer to Larry's place supported the idea of a group home and looked forward to the business it could bring. I had also found a few articles that dealt with scuffles between townspeople and some of the kids.

"Most of what's been reported is pretty negative," I said.

"Most of the time Larry keeps his kids in line," Mr. Hartford said. "They go about their business out there. They don't bother anybody. It's not news. But every now and then there's some kind of flare-up when a kid comes into town."

I'd read about that, too. Residents claimed that Larry had misled them. He'd said his kids would rarely, if ever, come to town. And at first their trips had been limited to once every couple of weeks, when Larry needed auto parts or hardware and came to town to get them. But over time that changed. Larry began to let the kids come to town once in a while for a treat. Once in a while turned into once a week.

"The times when there have been kids who got themselves into trouble or have taken off, those are the times when Larry's place makes the news."

"Taken off? You mean, ran away?"

He nodded. "Generally they seem to be kids who don't like the discipline out there. From some of the reaction around here, you'd think they were criminals making a prison break. People get nervous, check that their doors are locked, that kind of thing."

I thought about what Tal had said the night I'd gone into the ditch and what Bruno had said while he was walking me to my car. I also thought about what Nick had said—that kids like the ones out at Mr. Wilson's place could do things without thinking. Maybe some of them had run away because they didn't like the discipline. Or maybe they'd had other reasons for taking off, reasons that had something to do with whatever happened to Alex Richmond.

"News doesn't have to be all bad, does it?" I said to Mr. Hartford. "Maybe if the paper ran an article about the good work that Mr. Wilson is doing—"

"We're stretched pretty thin up here," Hartford said. "I know we seem like small potatoes compared to the big-city dailies, but our subscribers and advertisers have certain expectations, especially this time of year. It keeps Tom and Nan and me running."

"What if I did a story?" I said. "I could interview Mr. Wilson and talk to some of the kids out there, find out what they're learning and what they're planning to do with their lives."

"I don't know, Robyn. We may be small, but we try to practice solid journalism here. We don't do puff pieces."

"It wouldn't be a puff piece," I said quickly. "I could talk to people in town, too. I could get both sides of the story."

He looked doubtful.

"Tom said my story on the camp opening was pretty good," I said. "He made a few changes, but not many. He said I was a natural."

"I don't know . . ."

"I'll work on it on my own time."

He eyed me critically. "You're not interested in any of those boys, are you? Some of the girls around here seem to fall for those tough-guy types."

I shook my head. "I already have a boyfriend. I just think it could be a good story. I'd like to try it."

He thought for a moment. "What you do on your own time is your business. Go for it, if that's what you want. But I can't promise I'm going to print it."

"I understand."

. . .

"Great plan," Morgan said. We were boating our way across the lake to dock. She had called me late that afternoon to complain that she was bored. She asked me to come and get her so that we could have dinner in town.

After we ate, Morgan wanted to check out the local park. She had heard—don't ask me how; she seemed to have a special radar—that there was a soccer game going on and she was sure the place would be crawling with well-built guys. So we strolled down the main street. Or tried to—I had to keep slowing down to wait for Morgan, who was hobbling along beside me and grumbling about how her crutches were hurting her underarms and how her leg inside the cast was starting to itch and it was driving her crazy that she couldn't reach inside to scratch.

"Wait a minute, Robyn," she said—again.

I sighed, braced myself for more whining, and slowed down for what seemed like the hundredth time. Morgan had come to a complete stop and was gazing across the street.

"There's Nick," she said. "And that cute guy from the supermarket."

"That's Bruno. He's the one who rescued me from the ditch."

He was getting out of a pickup truck parked in front of an auto parts store. Nick was with him.

"Introduce me," Morgan begged.

"Does the name Billy ring a bell?"

"I just want to look. Please, Robyn?"

I sighed. It would give me a chance to get close to Nick. "All right. Come on."

I dashed across the street. Morgan hobbled after me with surprising speed.

"Bruno," I called.

He grinned when he saw me. "Hey, Robyn. Hi."

Morgan staggered to a halt beside me and eyed Bruno. I introduced them and then glanced at Nick, who was staring sullenly at me.

"I guess you guys haven't met," Bruno said. "Robyn, Morgan, this is Nick."

Nick nodded curtly at us.

A police car was coming down the street. I glanced at it, wondering if Dean Lafayette was behind the wheel.

But it was the other officer, the one who had searched the kid who had stolen the DVDs. He turned his head to look at Bruno and Nick as his car slid by.

"We were just on our way to watch a soccer game," I said to Bruno. "You guys want to come?"

"Can't," Bruno said. "We're here to pick up some parts, then we have to get back. Plus, soccer's not my game. We're in a baseball tournament a week from Sunday—Larry's kids against the volunteer fire department, all proceeds to the fire department. That's a game you won't want to miss."

"I'll keep it in mind," I said.

We stood there awkwardly for a moment. Bruno kept grinning at me. Nick kept scowling.

"Well," I said finally, "I guess we should let you two—"

"Robyn's doing a story on you guys for the newspaper," Morgan said.

"Yeah?" Bruno said. "I didn't know you were a reporter."

"I'm more like a gofer. The editor said I could try a story, but he didn't promise to publish it."

"And you want to do a story about us?"

"About Mr. Wilson and what he's doing. Who knows? Maybe if people get to know more about what goes on out there, they'll calm down a little."

"Maybe," Bruno said. "But I doubt it." He nudged Nick. "Come on. We gotta get going. Larry's waiting for those parts."

"God, he's cute," Morgan said after they'd gone inside. She was practically drooling.

Nick came out again a moment later carrying a heavy crate, which he slid into the back of the truck. As he turned to go back in the store, he hissed at me: "A newspaper article?"

"It was my idea," I said. "It will give me a chance to talk to Mr. Wilson and some of the kids out there. I want to help, Nick."

"I don't need your help. I want the guys to relax around me so I can find out what happened to Alex. People don't relax when there's a reporter around. Stay away from there, Robyn. I mean it."

Bruno came out, also carrying a heavy box. "Let's get a move on, Nick. There are a couple more crates in there."

Nick glowered at me as he pushed past into the store.

"That didn't work out too well," Morgan said as we made our way to the soccer game. She was right. I felt terrible. The last thing I wanted was for Nick to be mad at me.

"I guess I'll have to tell Mr. Hartford that I changed my mind," I said. "He probably won't mind. He wasn't keen on the idea in the first place."

CHAPTER **NINE**

"How's your story coming along, Robyn?" Mr. Hartford asked me the next morning.

"Well, actually, I wanted to talk to you about that," I said. "Maybe you're right. Maybe it isn't such a good idea."

"Nonsense. It's a terrific idea."

"But you said—"

"I ran into Larry Wilson last night at a Chamber of Commerce meeting. I told him what you wanted to do. He's all for it."

"Well, I—"

"I warned him," he continued. "I said that if we did a story, it would be balanced and objective, which means that we'd talk to his detractors as well as his supporters. He said he'd be glad to cooperate any way he could."

"Yes, but—"

"The mayor thinks it's a great idea too. So do some

93

of the local storeowners who do business with Larry. It's no secret that a lot of people don't like Larry and his kids, but his business and his group home are important to the towns around here. Take whatever time you need for your article, Robyn. If you need any help or advice, come to me or ask Tom. And give Larry a call to set up an interview. He's expecting to hear from you." He bustled away to his office. I stared helplessly after him. When I turned to go to my desk, Tom grinned at me.

"Nice work, Scoop," he said.

I wondered what Nick would say. I wondered if he would be angry with me. I wished he would get in touch so that I could tell him.

I lay awake that night, listening and hoping that Nick would swim across the lake again so that I could talk to him.

He didn't.

. . .

The next morning, Mr. Hartford asked me if I'd set up an interview with Larry Wilson yet. I had no choice. I called, and Mr. Wilson invited me out to his place the next day.

Wilson was waiting for me when I pulled up to his gate that afternoon. He walked me around the compound and took me through the bunkhouse—a long, gleaming building that contained six small but sparkling-clean double rooms, three bathrooms, and a lounge equipped with a TV, a DVD player, and a lot of framed photographs on the wall. The faces in them were all male, all young. "Some of the alumni," Mr. Wilson said. Some of the guys in the pictures were hard at work and covered in grease; some were fooling around on a dock; one was standing next to Mr. Wilson, holding up a string of fish.

"Pickerel," Mr. Wilson said. "We cooked them up that night. There's nothing like fish fresh from the water. Even the kids who swore they didn't like fish went back for seconds."

There was a classroom building equipped with old computer equipment. "Some of the boys are finishing high school online," Wilson told me. "At first I tried enrolling them in the nearest public school. But there were only ever a couple of the boys who were interested, and they weren't exactly welcomed with open arms. Some teachers were hostile. Some of the local kids picked fights with them—and my kids were the ones who always ended up being punished. It was counterproductive. So I recruited a couple of teachers I used to work with. They come here for a few days every month, help the kids with whatever I can't help them with, and leave them with assignments."

There was an enormous garden behind the classroom building. Two boys, slick with sweat, were working in it. One was pulling weeds. The other was working the soil with a hoe.

"You name it, we grow it—tomatoes, lettuce, beans, peas, potatoes, corn, carrots, peppers," Mr. Wilson said.

"Most of these kids have never eaten fresh produce regularly. The ones who've spent a lot of time on the street have really bad eating habits. I don't stock junk food. If they want something sweet, they have to bake it themselves. Hot dogs are on the menu a couple of times a year—we have the occasional wiener roast. The rest of the time it's home-cooked. By the time the boys leave they know how to prepare a balanced meal. And that doesn't hurt when it comes to the ladies." He winked at me.

From there, we got into an old Jeep to tour the property. Back a couple of miles from the house was a huge scrapyard. Bruno, Derek, and two other boys whose names I didn't know were working there.

"I get a lot of salvage—cars that have been abandoned or that are in such bad shape that the owners can't sell them," Wilson said. "We strip off the parts that have cash value and sell the rest for scrap metal."

We drove a little farther along a dirt road that ran through increasingly dense woods. "There's a small lake over there," Wilson said. I saw a shimmer of blue in the distance. "It's not big, but it's deep. The boys go swimming there." I wondered if that was where Alex Richmond had died. We came to a fork in the road, and Mr. Wilson turned the Jeep around.

"What's that way?" I said, pointing in the direction we hadn't taken.

"Some old sheds, a cookhouse, a bunkhouse—all pretty run-down—from back when this area was being logged. And that way"—he pointed down the other road—"is an abandoned logging road that runs clear up to Wild River Road. It's pretty rough, though, even for the Jeep. There's an old sawmill back there, right near the Wild River. It's abandoned now, but it's not in bad shape. Every now and again I try to interest the county in restoring the place—it'd make a great tourist attraction. You could turn it into a museum of logging. But—" He shrugged. "It's all about money. And plenty of people up here say I only push the idea so I can make money off it, even though I've offered more than once to donate the land to the county."

"Maybe I'll put that in my article," I said. "I met the woman who runs the local historical society."

Mr. Wilson smiled at me. "If even one of the locals was as enthusiastic as you are, maybe these kids would have a chance to really join the community."

While we drove back to the main compound, I asked him about some of the kids who had lived at his group home.

"What happens to them after they leave?"

"A couple of the boys—the ones who were the oldest when I started—are working as mechanics," he said. "A couple went back to school—first to finish high school, then to upgrade their skills."

"So they've all been success stories?"

"I wish I could say yes," he said. "But that wouldn't be the truth. You can only do your best, Robyn. The first thing these kids have to learn is discipline. You can't be part of a team—I don't care if that team is your family, your co-workers, your friends—if you don't have the discipline to play by the rules. A lot of these kids have spent most of their lives running wild or willfully breaking the rules. I don't let them get away with that up here. If they're going to succeed, they have to be willing to meet me halfway. I interview the kids before I take them in. I try to pick the ones who are most in need of the type of program I'm running and who I think have the best chance to succeed—but I don't always choose correctly."

"Do you think I could interview some of the guys for my story?"

He glanced at me. "I can't force them to answer your questions. But you're free to ask for volunteers. Just don't be surprised if you don't get too many takers. These kids have had mostly bad experiences with the press, especially up here."

"But I want to give them a chance to tell their side of the story."

"Tell you what," Mr. Wilson said. "Stay for dinner. Let them get to know you a little. Then we'll ask them, see if anyone is interested. How about it?"

It sounded like a plan.

. . .

When I walked into the kitchen with Mr. Wilson, the boys who were preparing supper fell silent. Wilson introduced me and told them to set an extra place at the table. He grabbed a large bell from the top of the fridge, opened the back door, and stepped outside. A few minutes later, boys started filing into the kitchen. They all stared at me. One by one they fell silent. Nick was one of the last ones into the room. He didn't look at all surprised to see me. He must have seen me touring the property with Mr. Wilson.

Wilson stood at one end of the table. "Why don't you sit here, Robyn?" he said, pulling out the chair to the right of where he was standing.

I sat down. Mr. Wilson nodded, and fifteen chairs scraped against the linoleum as the boys all took their seats. Bruno anchored the other end of the table. Nick was seated next to me. He didn't look at me even once. I desperately wished I could explain that I had tried to drop the story. Even if I did tell him, I wondered if he would believe me.

Bowls and platters of food were passed around. Each boy took only a modest portion. Then, as they started to eat, Wilson asked one of them how the garden was coming along. During the course of the meal he engaged each boy in conversation at least once. Things loosened up a little, too. Guys teased each other and made jokes. It was almost as if they had forgotten I was there. Well, maybe not everyone. As the plates from the main course were being cleared away, I felt Nick's hand on my knee. I slid my own hand under the table, and Nick pressed something into it. A note. I slipped it into my pocket.

"Raspberries, Robyn?" Mr. Wilson said. "Eddie picked them this afternoon. Later in the summer we'll have fresh blueberries."

I accepted eagerly. The berries were juicy and fragrant, and they were topped with a dollop of whipped cream.

When the meal was over Mr. Wilson said, "Before the clean-up crew gets started, Robyn here has a request. She's working on a story about us for the local paper—"

A couple of guys groaned. Someone whispered something to the kid next to him.

"Manners, guys," Mr. Wilson said, holding up a hand. "I showed Robyn around the place today and answered all of her questions. She wants to do a balanced story on what goes on up here, and she asked me if she could interview some of you. So, what do you say? Volunteers?"

Nobody said a word. I looked around the table. The only person who met my eyes was Bruno, and he shook his head. I turned to Mr. Wilson. He shrugged his regret.

"If any of you change your mind," he said, "let me know, and I'll tell Robyn." He excused himself from the table and stood up. "Let me walk you to your car." On the way he said, "I'm sorry you didn't get more cooperation. But you can't say I didn't warn you. It takes long enough for these kids to trust me and each other . . ."

"It's okay. I understand." I thanked him for his help. When I left the compound, I had to remind myself to drive within the speed limit. But it was hard because Nick's note was burning a hole in my pocket. As soon as I parked at the marina, I dug it out and unfolded it. It said "Supermarket. 10 A.M. Tomorrow."

. . .

I spotted the black pickup truck before I made the turn into the grocery-store parking lot the next morning.

"I told you we were going to be late," I said to Morgan.

"You try rushing when you're on crutches," she snapped at me. "I didn't even have time for a cup of coffee." One more reason she was in such a rotten mood. "I don't understand why you're in such a hurry. He's probably just going to yell at you for going out there again."

She was probably right. But at least I would have a chance to explain.

"You didn't have to come," I said.

"I'm getting tired of sitting around out there all by myself while you have all the fun. I've read all my magazines. There's no place decent to shop around here. I can't go swimming. I can't play mini golf. I can't go hiking. I can't do anything."

"We'll rent some movies before we go back to the marina."

"I'm tired of movies. I'm bored out of my mind. My leg itches all the time. And I miss Billy. This is the worst summer I've ever had."

"You can wait here if you want, Morgan."

"No way. Maybe Bruno will be with him."

"You just said you missed Billy."

"I do! Which is why it would be nice to have a guy to talk to." She flung the passenger side door open and shoved her crutches out ahead of her. "Coming?"

I circled the car and helped Morgan to her feet. We got a shopping cart from the front of the store and patrolled the aisles until we found Nick. He was in the baking section, checking out a display of herbs and spices.

"Hey," I said.

"Hey." He nodded at Morgan and then glanced over his shoulder. It was impossible to tell what he was thinking. "You're late. Derek went across the street to pick up some paint. He should be back any minute."

"Nick, I'm sorry about coming up with that idea—"

Nick pulled me closer.

"I'm not positive, Robyn, but I get the feeling they're watching me."

"Who's watching you?"

"Larry, Derek, Bruno. I think there's something going on out there, Robyn. Alex isn't the only kid who has died."

"What?" Morgan and I said in unison.

Nick glanced at both ends of the aisle again.

"Morgan, go watch the door," I said. "Signal if you see Derek."

"Who's Derek?" Morgan said.

"Tall, well-built, brown hair down to his collar," I said.

"He's got a skull-and-crossbones tat on his left forearm," Nick said. "You can't miss it."

As Morgan crutched her way up the aisle, I said, "What do you mean, Alex isn't the only kid who's died?"

"There's this kid out there, his name is Lucas."

"The one who got caught stealing from that store," I said.

"Yeah. He's the one who told me. There's another kid who died out there. He sounded really nervous, Robyn."

"Nervous? About what?"

"He wouldn't say. But you know what else he said? First chance he gets, he's going to do a break-and-enter, a smash-and-grab, something like that."

"He told you he's going to commit a crime? Doesn't he realize he could get sent back to the city, put back in custody?"

"I get the feeling that's the point," Nick said grimly. "I think he wants to get away from here any way he can."

"Why? What's going on?"

"I don't know. But something is. I can feel it. The past couple days, everyone's been guarded. A couple of times when I walked into a room, people stopped talking. Something's not right. I think Lucas knows it, too. I think that's why he wants to get out."

"We should talk to the police, Nick."

He shook his head. "That's the other thing. There's this cop I've seen out there a few times. He's kind of creepy, always wearing sunglasses and gloves. Like something out of a bad movie. I've seen him talking to Larry. I think there's something going on between the two of them."

"You're saying a cop is in on whatever it is that you think is going on?"

"I don't think something's going on, Robyn. I know it. I just don't know what it is yet. And for sure I don't trust the cops."

"If you're right," I said—and, believe me, I was skeptical—"if there is something going on, then it could be dangerous. Maybe I should call my dad."

"No," Nick said firmly. "I don't want you to do anything, Robyn. I promised Seth I was going to find out what happened to Alex, and that's what I'm going to do. I want you to stay away from there, okay? Drop the story idea, just to be on the safe side."

"I tried to. But Mr. Hartford—he's the editor—said—"

"Find a way, Robyn. Drop it."

"What about you? Are you going to be okay?"

"They're checking me out. I think they check everyone out. If I play it right, I'm pretty sure I can get them to trust me enough so that I can find out what happened to Alex. Then I'm out of there. I don't want any trouble, believe me."

"But what if it's dangerous?"

"I can take care of myself. Besides, you're here. I'll try to keep in touch with you."

"Try?"

"That way, if anything happens to me—"

I thought about Alex and the other dead kid, and I felt sick inside.

"Nick, maybe it's not such a good idea—"

I heard a loud crash and looked up. Cans of baked beans rolled past the top of the aisle.

"Ohmygod!" Morgan said in a loud voice. "Did I do that?"

"Derek," I said. I glanced at Nick.

"Go," he said.

I hesitated.

He gave me a little push, propelling me up the aisle. I kept moving until I found Morgan, crutchless, surrounded by dozens of cans of beans and being helped to her feet by a guy with brown, collar-length hair, and a skull-and-crossbones tattoo on his left forearm. Derek. Morgan was beaming at him.

"Are you okay?" I said.

She nodded without even glancing at me. She was too busy smiling blissfully at her rescuer.

"Hi, Derek," I said. "I see you've met my friend Morgan."

"Hey, Robyn," Derek bent and picked up Morgan's crutches for her. Then he excused himself.

"Wow," Morgan said. "He's even cuter than Bruno. What are they running out there? A stud farm?"

"Very funny," I said.

"Who's kidding?" Morgan said.

CHAPTER **TEN**

"Come on," Morgan said. "What could they possibly be up to out there?"

"I don't know. But I'm going to help Nick find out."

"I thought you said he told you to stay out of it."

"What if he's right? What if there really is something going on? What if he's in danger?"

"What are you planning to do, Robyn?"

"I'm going to keep working on my story. Mr. Hartford told me I had to be objective. So I'm going to talk to people in town. Maybe someone knows something."

"Why don't you talk to the police chief? He's your dad's friend. I'm sure he could answer your questions."

"Maybe I will," I said, even though Nick had told me not to. If there's one thing I've learned from my father, it's that there are many different ways to ask questions. It all depends on who you're talking to and what you want to know.

I left Morgan sitting at a patio café with a large latte and a couple of new magazines. She had offered to go with me, but "Reporters don't take their friends on assignment, Morgan. Besides, you don't want to traipse all over town on those crutches."

"Do I look like I could traipse even if I wanted to?" she said irritably.

"I'll be back as soon as I can."

Be objective, Mr. Hartford had said. Larry Wilson had given me one side of the story—his side. But it was obvious that he had a lot of detractors in town. I decided to talk to some of them, starting with someone I was sure would have a strong opinion.

"Excuse me, Mr. Kastner?" I said to the man in the record store who was putting price stickers on a new shipment of albums.

"How can I help you?" he said. His smile was warm and welcoming. He didn't look anything like the angry man who had chased Lucas out of the store. Not until I told him why I was there. His smile vanished and his warm eyes turned cold. "Thugs," he said bitterly. "Not the kind of kids we need around here."

"Have they given you a lot of trouble?"

"Those two who were in here the week before last— I had my eye on them from the minute they walked through the door. I knew they were trouble. Although, if you ask me, they're not too smart. Especially that one I caught."

"What do you mean?"

"He went straight to the new releases and started pawing through them. The whole time he kept glancing at me, like he was trying to see if I was watching him or not. It was obvious he was up to something. He didn't even get his friend to try to distract me—I've had some kids like that before, in pairs or groups, a couple of them trying to distract me while the others lift the merchandise."

I remembered what Nick had told me about Lucas. "But the kids who were in here a week ago didn't do that?"

"While the guilty-looking one was going through the new releases, his friend was studying the flyers on the wall. He didn't check even once to see what I was doing."

"Then what happened?"

"While I was watching, the kid who was going through the DVDs slipped a couple of them into the back of his pants under that big T-shirt he was wearing. I've never seen such a clumsy attempt at shoplifting. Then he ran out of the store. Even if I hadn't been watching him, that would have tipped me off.

"I yelled at my wife to call the cops—she was in the back of the store—then I chased him and caught him. Then out comes his friend, yelling at me that the kid hadn't done anything." He snorted in contempt. "I should have made the police throw the book at that thief. Next time one of those little thugs comes into my store, that's exactly what I'm going to do."

"So they've given you a lot of trouble?" I said.

"Like I just told you."

"Before that, I mean. Have you had trouble from some of Mr. Wilson's other kids?"

"Well, no," he said. "Not Wilson's kids personally, I mean. But plenty of other people around here have."

"What kind of trouble?"

"Last summer they used to come into town in a big group and muscle their way into the ice cream shop. Intimidated the other customers."

"Intimidated them? How?"

"Well, they're delinquents," he said, as if the answer to my question was perfectly obvious. "Bert Olafson, the owner, had to ban them from the place."

It sounded to me like people were intimidated because they knew that Wilson's kids had been in trouble before, not because of anything they did in the ice cream shop.

"You know who you should talk to for your article?" Kastner said. "Al Duggan at the marina. He had some real trouble with one of those kids. He'll tell you a story or two."

I thanked him for his time and went back to the café to find Morgan, who was sharing her table with a cute, shorthaired guy she introduced as Chris.

"Chris's dad is a contractor. He builds those big

luxury cabins you see on a lot of the lakes up here." Before Chris could say anything, she added, "Chris has a Sea-Doo." She smiled at him.

"Too bad you can't get that cast wet," I said. She scowled. "I'm going down to the marina. You want to come?"

She gazed across the table at Chris. "No. I think I'll stay here."

"I'll come by and get you when I'm finished."

I headed down to the marina and asked around for Al Duggan.

"He's in the restaurant," a kid at the gas pumps told me.

On my way inside I passed Al Duggan's daughter Colleen, who had helped me dock the first time I crossed the lake on my own. She was writing the daily specials on a menu board outside the restaurant and nodded at me as I went by. I found Mr. Duggan inside, behind the register. When I introduced myself and told him why I was there, he reacted the same way as Kastner at the music store.

"I'm surprised Rob Hartford is wasting ink on those punks," he said. "I'm not sure his advertisers will want to open the paper and see their ads next to a story on Larry Wilson."

"That's why I wanted to talk to you," I said. "Mr. Hartford wants me to cover both sides of the story, and I heard you've had problems with some of Mr. Wilson's kids."

"No respect for anyone else's property," he said. "One of them stole some DVDs from George Kastner's store last week."

"What kind of trouble did you have with them?"

"One of those thugs destroyed a pay phone over there." He nodded toward the door. "Cracked a window, too—I had to have it replaced. I pressed charges, but Larry sweet-talked the chief of police into giving the kid a warning. I told him the next time any of those kids set foot on my property they'd be asked to leave. If they didn't . . ." His grimace made his intentions clear.

"Have they given you any other trouble?"

"They used to come in here, a whole bunch of them all at once. They'd shove a bunch of tables together, order some fries and soda, and hang around for an hour or more, annoying the other customers."

"They weren't any worse than J.C. and some of the other kids from school," someone said. We both turned toward the door. Colleen had a bucket of chalk in her hand. It was obvious that she had been listening to us.

"J.C. doesn't have a criminal record," Mr. Duggan said.

"You don't have to have a criminal record to act like a bunch of jerks. Which J.C. and his friends do all the time when they're in here," Colleen said. "But when they act up, you just tell them to knock it off. You don't threaten to call the cops."

"That's because I don't have to worry that J.C. is going to pull out a knife or that he's going to come back in the middle of the night and trash the place."

"Steven would never have done anything like that," Colleen said.

Steven? Who was Steven?

"The lunch rush starts in half an hour," Mr. Duggan said. "Everything had better be prepped back there, or your mom's not going to be happy."

Colleen glowered at her dad for a moment before disappearing into the kitchen.

"Do you know of any storeowners in town who have had a positive experience with Larry Wilson's kids?"

"Not a one," Duggan said without hesitation. "Nobody wanted those kids to move up here. Nobody wants their children hanging out with them. One way or another, this town is going to shut that place down."

I thanked him for his time. I was beginning to understand that this was going to be a hard story to write. So far the townspeople I had spoken to came off sounding worse than Mr. Wilson's kids. Okay, maybe they had some grievances—Lucas had shoplifted, albeit clumsily, and another kid had done some damage at the marina restaurant. But Mr. Kastner and Mr. Duggan talked about those incidents as if they were crimes of the century.

When I got back to the café where I had left Morgan, she was alone.

"Where's Sea-Doo Boy?" I said.

She gave me a sour look. "With his girlfriend, who, by the way, has obvious self-esteem issues. The way she acted, you'd have thought I was trying to steal Chris. I guess these local girls aren't used to competition."

"Competition?" I said. "You mean you were trying to steal him?"

"We were just *talking*, Robyn. It's not my fault that he was enjoying himself."

I stared at her.

"What?" she said.

"Billy," I said.

"I have the cutest, most comfortable pair of boots at home," she said. I knew the ones she meant. She practically lived in them when the weather got cold.

"Relevance?"

"Those boots are irreplaceable. Nothing even comes close. I wouldn't sell them or give them away—ever. But that doesn't mean I can't go window shopping just for fun. Anyway, I was doing you a favor."

"Me? I'm not in the market for new boots either, Morgan."

"But you are in the market for information about Larry's kids. When I told Chris why you were going to the marina, he said you should talk to Colleen Duggan."

"Did he say why?"

"Colleen went out with one of those kids. The guy's name was Steven. And Robyn?" Morgan's expression was somber. "Chris said that he's dead."

"Dead?" Lucas had told Nick that Alex Richmond wasn't the only one of Mr. Wilson's kids who had died. "Did he say what happened?"

"He got lost in the woods. He died of exposure."

"When did this happen?"

"Last winter."

I frowned. "Are you sure? I went through all the back issues of the *Lakesider*. I saw a story about Alex Richmond's death, but I didn't see anything about a kid dying of exposure."

"I'm just telling you what Chris said. And I didn't get the impression that he was making it up."

"Come on," I said.

"Where are we going?"

"I hear they make a good burger down at the marina restaurant. And we haven't had lunch."

. . .

Al Duggan hadn't been kidding about the lunch rush. By the time Morgan and I got back to the marina, the restaurant was jammed. Colleen was one of only two waitresses, but she wasn't ours. Morgan and I ordered and lingered over our lunches. Gradually the place cleared out as vacationers headed out to one of the nearby beaches, climbed back into their boats, or strolled into town.

"Can I get you anything else?" our waitress said.

I glanced around but didn't see Colleen anywhere.

"No, we're good," I said. After she left, I told Morgan I would be right back. I headed for the washroom but peeked through the kitchen door. No Colleen.

We paid for our meal and left the restaurant, then started toward the dock.

"Hey!" someone called.

I turned.

It was Colleen. She was behind the restaurant, beckoning to me.

"I want to talk to you about something," she said. "I have a break in twenty minutes. Meet me at the bandstand on the beach. You know where it is?"

"I do," Morgan said.

It took us almost the whole twenty minutes to get there. It turns out it isn't easy to walk over sand when you're on crutches.

"Three more weeks," Morgan grumbled. "And then this stupid cast comes off." A little later: "There's sand in it. I can feel it. It's going to drive me crazy."

"You don't have to come, Morgan. You can wait for me at the marina."

"Stop babying me, Robyn. I'm here, aren't I? I'm fine." She didn't sound fine. "Besides, we're almost there."

Colleen showed up a few minutes later.

"I heard you talking to my dad," she said. "You're doing a story on Larry's kids?"

I nodded.

"Are you going to write what my dad said?"

"About Steven, you mean?"

Her eyes filled with tears.

"I heard he died, Colleen."

She wiped her hand across her cheeks and drew in a deep breath.

"He was nice," she said. "Sweet, you know?"

"Your dad said he vandalized the restaurant."

"I know what he said. He tells everyone the same thing. But that's not what happened. Steven came into the restaurant last fall. The marina slows down after Labor Day. By Thanksgiving it closes. But Dad keeps the restaurant open year-round. There's a lot of winter sports up here—ice fishing, snowmobiling, cross-country skiing. That keeps us afloat. I usually have to help out after school and on weekends. Dad likes to keep as much money as possible in the family. Anyway, one afternoon I was there. The place was practically deserted, and this guy came in."

"Steven?"

She nodded. "He was looking for a phone. There's an ancient pay phone just inside the door. I was sitting in a booth, doing homework. My dad was in the kitchen. I saw Steven, but I don't think he saw me at first. He was making a long-distance call. I know because he tried to reverse the charges. But whoever he was calling refused to accept. I heard him arguing with the operator. He kept saying it was important. But it didn't do any good. He hung up, but he didn't leave. He just stood there. He looked kind of sad, you know? So I got a bunch of change out of the till and I gave it to him so he could make his call.

"At first he didn't want to accept it. But he finally

took the money and made his call. I couldn't hear what he was saying at first—he was hunched over the phone, and I was sitting in a back booth, you know, to give him some privacy. But I guess the call didn't go the way he wanted, 'cause he started to talk really loud."

"What was he saying?"

"He wanted to go home."

"You mean he wanted to leave Mr. Wilson's place?"

She nodded again. "What my dad said, about how he broke the phone, then the window? He makes it sound like Steven just came in and started smashing the place up. But it wasn't like that. Steven was begging whoever he was talking to to let him leave."

"Did he say why he wanted to go?"

"If he did, I didn't hear it. But I did hear him promise that he'd be good, that he wouldn't make any trouble, stuff like that. Then all of a sudden he was just standing there, staring at the receiver like he got hung up on. Then he slammed it down—hard. I guess he was really upset, because he did it again and again. My dad came out of the kitchen to see what was going on, and just then Steven slammed the receiver down so hard that it broke.

"Dad grabbed him by the collar. Steven fought back. I mean, wouldn't you if someone grabbed you all of a sudden and started screaming at you? Dad was shouting, getting really scary. Even I wasn't sure if he was going to hit Steven or something. Steven tried to get free of him. I guess he pushed my dad, because Dad slammed against the window—it got this huge crack in it. But Steven didn't run away or anything like that. He tried to help Dad up. But Dad shoved him away. Steven tried to apologize. My dad wouldn't listen. He called the cops."

"What did Steven do?"

"He didn't do anything."

"He didn't take off before the cops came?"

"Nope. He just stood there while my dad called him a loser, told him he was going to be sorry he ever set foot in the restaurant, stuff like that. Then Chief Lafayette showed up. He handcuffed Steven and took a statement from my dad, and that was it. It wasn't the way Dad told you. I wanted you to know. I didn't want you to write what my dad said."

"Your dad told me that Mr. Wilson got the charges against Steven dropped," I said.

Colleen nodded. "You can't believe how angry Dad was when he heard. He made banned the rest of Mr. Wilson's kids from the place. He said he had half a mind to ban the police from the restaurant, too." When I looked puzzled, she said, "The police station is right across the road. Chief Lafayette and his deputy are regulars. One comes in on chicken night, the other comes in whenever my mom makes her special meatloaf. My dad liked having them around. He still does. He says when people see cops eating there, they know it's a good place. A place where there's no trouble. But he was pretty mad when Chief Lafayette let Steven off with a warning."

"It sounds like a lot of people in town don't like

Larry's kids," I said.

"That's for sure. Maybe some of those kids are trouble, I don't know. But Steven wasn't bad. A little while after he was in the restaurant, I was walking home from school and I saw Steven on the road. He was waiting for me. He wanted to pay back the money I had given him from the till. He said he was sorry for breaking the phone. If he was such a punk, he wouldn't have bothered apologizing."

Steven sounded a lot like Nick—sure, he had a temper, but apart from that he was a decent person.

"Did you see him again after that?"

She looked away.

"I won't put it in my story, Colleen. I promise."

"Then why do you want to know?"

I hesitated and glanced at Morgan, who shook her head.

"I went out to Larry Wilson's place a couple of times," I said. "It seems like a good place. The guys out there seemed well behaved. They're learning all kinds of things. They work hard. But when I talk to people in town . . ."

"If I tell you, you have to promise you won't write about it," Colleen said.

"I promise."

"Mr. Wilson lets the guys come to town once a week—usually Thursday afternoon. They mostly have to stay in pairs or groups, and he's really strict about the time. Steven said he's strict about everything. But—the guy Steven used to pair up with would sometimes let Steven go off on his own. Steven said he thought the guy was seeing someone in town. So Steven would come and see me."

"At the marina?"

"You kidding? And take the chance he'd run into my dad? After that first time, when he paid me back, I told him I would be at the library on Thursdays. We'd meet there and then find somewhere more private where we could talk. Steven was nice. He just wanted to go home—not that he had much of a home to go to."

"Did he have problems with his parents?"

"He didn't have parents. He didn't have anyone. No brothers or sisters. No uncles, aunts, grandparents, not a single person in the world. Can you imagine what that must have been like?"

After knowing Nick for as long as I had, I sort of could. "What kind of home did he have?"

"He was in foster care with some other kids. He was talking to his foster parents on the phone that day. But they didn't want him back. Steven said they weren't the greatest people. He said he thought they just did it for the money. They told him they had no room for him, that he was better off where he was. I think he felt like nobody wanted him."

"Then why would he want to go back?" Morgan asked.

"He said he didn't like it out at Larry's place."

"Did he say what he didn't like about it?" I asked.

"He didn't want to talk about it. He just said he didn't like what was happening out there and that he'd rather be back in the city, even if it meant trying to make it on his own."

"We heard he got lost in the woods. Do you know how that happened?"

"Yeah. He told me he was going to leave. He said he'd get in touch with me as soon as he got settled in the city. After that, I didn't hear from him for weeks. I was so worried. Then I heard someone say that one of Larry's kids had run away. By the time they found him he'd frozen to death. He was such a city kid. They said he wasn't dressed right to be in the woods in the middle of winter. And it can be confusing out there if you're not used to it. All those trees look pretty much the same, and everything was covered with snow. They said he'd been walking in circles." A tear trickled down her cheek.

"I didn't see anything in the paper about it," I said after a few moments.

"At first Mr. Wilson didn't tell anyone that Steven had run away. I heard he was afraid how people would react. You know what they think of those kids. And then when he was found—" She wiped away a few more tears. "He was found on Mr. Henderson's resort."

"The ski place?" Morgan said.

Colleen nodded. "One of the trail groomers found him. My dad knows Mr. Henderson really well. My dad said he freaked when the cops told him what they'd found. He pressured Mr. Griffith at the newspaper not to mention it. He said, it's not like anyone cares—and that it could be bad for business, you know, all those city people hearing that they found a body at the resort . . ." More tears ran down her cheeks. "Do you believe that? It's like Mr. Henderson was right. Nobody cared."

"You cared," I said.

"For all the good it did." She wiped her tears away with the palms of her hands. "I have to get back." She stood up. "Remember," she said. "You promised." She started to walk away.

"Hey, Colleen?"

She turned.

"The guy Steven used to come into town with—the one who used to let him go off on his own. Was he meeting a girl?" If he was, maybe I could talk to her.

"I don't know. Steven never said, and I never asked."

"Do you know the guy's name?" It might help Nick if he knew that one of Larry's kids had been breaking the rules. Maybe he could get the guy to talk to him.

Colleen shook her head.

CHAPTER **ELEVEN**

The next morning, Morgan was up before me. She was out behind the house, wearing rubber kitchen gloves and balancing on one crutch while she did her best to clean up the garbage that was strewn around the garbage cans.

"What happened?" I said.

"I'm hoping it was raccoons. But I'm afraid it might have been a bear."

"A bear? What makes you say that? Did you see it?"

"I didn't even hear it. Did you?"

I shook my head.

"But I did hear the radio first thing this morning, Robyn. A woman was walking in the woods behind her cottage before dark. She ran into a bear. She did all the right things. At first she backed away and watched the bear, hoping that it would leave. But the bear kept coming toward her. It said on the news that at one point the bear was less than six feet away from her."

"What did she do?"

"She did what they tell you to do when a bear approaches."

"Which is?"

"For the kind of bears around here, you're supposed to stop and face the bear. Do not run. Then you wave your arms to make yourself look bigger and make noise—you know, be aggressive and try to get the bear to leave."

I looked into the thick woods behind Morgan's summerhouse.

"What happened to the woman?"

"She finally managed to get into her house. The bear prowled around outside for more than half an hour. She called the police. They called some rangers. But by the time they got there, the bear was gone."

I wasn't sure I wanted to ask my next question: "Where did this happen?"

"Just down the point."

"You think the same bear got into our garbage?"

"Maybe. But I think we should be careful with our garbage. I'm afraid of bears, Robyn. Especially ones that aren't afraid of people."

"No problem." I glanced around nervously. "I'll get another pair of gloves."

We cleaned up quickly, both of us checking the yard and the tree line obsessively, afraid we would see a bear lumbering toward us.

. . .

Lunch detail turned out to be my most predictable duty at the *Lakesider*. Every day at quarter to noon I made the rounds of the staff and collected orders and money from everyone who was planning to work through lunch, which turned out most days to be everyone except Mr. Griffith. I'm not exactly sure what newspaper publishers do. I only know that whatever it is, they do it outside of their office more often than they do it in their office. I always went to the same place—Roxy's. I was sitting on a stool at the lunch counter, waiting for the order, when someone said, "Robyn, how's it going?"

I spun around. It was Dean Lafayette. He was smiling at me.

"It's going fine," I said.

"Are you enjoying the job?"

"Yes. Well, except maybe for these lunch runs."

He laughed. "Everybody starts somewhere. I hear they've given you a couple of interesting assignments. Rob tells me you're working on a piece about Larry's kids. What sparked your interest in that?"

I told him about my accident and how a couple of Mr. Wilson's guys had helped me out. I also told him that I thought there was a big discrepancy between what it was like at Mr. Wilson's place and how people in town regarded the kids.

"Discrepancy?"

"Everyone's so negative about Larry's kids. It seems unfair."

"Tell me about it." He settled on the stool next to mine. "I get more complaints about those kids than about anything else. More often than not, the complaints are blown out of proportion. I'm not saying those kids are perfect. But I can't tell you the number of times I answer a call from one of the local storeowners asking me to move those kids away from the sidewalk in front of his place. Or to kick kids out of his shop, even though all the kids want is to buy something. At first I argued with them—you can't stop people from coming into your place to shop. But I seem to be fighting a losing battle. If I don't try to move those kids out, people do it themselves—and that usually makes the problem even worse. Larry's been pretty cooperative, all things considered. He's made peace with some of the storeowners—the ones who benefit most from his business, the grocery store and the hardware store. He's tried to keep his kids out of the way of the people who are less understanding. He's even tried his hand at public relations."

"Public relations? What do you mean?"

"Last year his kids participated in a walk-a-thon to raise money for the conservation area. They couldn't collect pledges from the locals, of course. So they canvassed the tourists and the cottagers. People usually collect the money for those things up front, but Larry had his kids do it differently. They collected pledges only, no cash. Then, once they completed the walk, the mayor signed their pledge forms, you know, to show that they had actually done the walk. Then they went back door-to-door with the executive director of the conservation area, and people gave the pledges directly to him. Those kids raised more than a thousand dollars."

"I didn't see anything about that in the newspaper."

"A pileup on the highway resulted in an oil spill, and that pushed that story out of the *Lakesider*," he said. It sounded to me like he didn't think that was the real reason the story hadn't made the paper. I remembered what Colleen had said about the resort owner pressuring the paper not to print the story about Steven.

"This year Larry has organized a softball game—his guys against the volunteer fire department. The fire department is selling tickets for the game, and all the proceeds go to them. I understand sales have been pretty brisk. In my opinion, there are a lot of people in town who want to see those kids get their clocks cleaned at the game."

"Sounds as though Mr. Wilson's public relations moves aren't working out," I said.

Dean Lafayette sighed. "The people up here aren't so bad, Robyn. They just see things a certain way. They like their town. It's nice. It's clean. It's safe. Relatively crime-free. There hasn't been a homicide up here for years. And they don't like the idea that they're getting saddled with someone else's problem. Larry's kids are all products of the city. They think the city should deal with them. But they're also fair people. If Larry's kids stay out of trouble, folks might eventually get used having them around. They might even get to know some of those kids and find out what I already know—that, for the most part, they're regular kids who have made a few wrong choices. That it's too soon to write them off."

I knew Nick didn't trust the police. He had very little reason to. But this was different. Dean Lafayette was my dad's friend. He cared about Larry's kids. And I didn't even have to mention Nick. I already had the perfect excuse to ask questions.

"I read back issues of the *Lakesider*," I said. "I saw an article about a kid who drowned at Larry Wilson's place."

"The suicide." He shook his head. "I was out of town when it happened. Phil handled the investigation—Phil Varton, my deputy. Coroner ruled it a suicide. Apparently the poor kid was depressed. His brother—his only family—was terminally ill. I guess he had trouble coping. Who wouldn't?"

"So it was definitely suicide? You're sure it couldn't have been something else? Some kind of fight or grudge? I've heard that guys like those can have a lot of problems. Or maybe—"

He looked surprised for a moment. Then he laughed. "You're Mac's daughter, all right. They tell you at the academy, a good cop has to be naturally suspicious. Can't assume anything. Mac was the most suspicious cop I know. Mind you, he was good at his job, too, which I guess is why he was so keen to make detective. Me, I'm more of a community-oriented type. I love the small-town life. I love that I know everybody who lives here year-round. I'm pretty good with the regular summer people too. But, to answer your question: Phil did a thorough death investigation, and the coroner was satisfied, so I'm satisfied."

"Has anybody ever mentioned anything to you about something . . . strange going on out at Mr. Wilson's place?" I said.

"Strange? What do you mean?"

"Well, people in town treat the kids out there like they're criminals. I was just wondering if that's because they think there might be some kind of criminal activity going on out there."

Dean Lafayette laughed again. "To be honest, it wouldn't surprise me. I mean, it wouldn't surprise me that some people might *think* that. As far as I know, all Larry Wilson is doing out there is turning lives around. In that sense, he's doing us all a favor, even if people around here don't want to give him credit for it."

The waitress came with my order, boxed and ready to go.

"Good luck with your story, Robyn," Dean Lafayette said. "And if there's anything I can do to help—not just about that, anything at all—just let me know."

. . .

"Robyn, run this ad over to Fred Brookner at the Hardware Emporium and have him approve it, will you?" Gloria said later that day. "He can't open our attachments, and I need his sign-off this afternoon."

I walked the three blocks to the hardware store and was told I would find Brookner in the lumberyard behind the store. I headed down a narrow aisle that had light fixtures on one side and packages of every conceivable type and size of nail and screw on the other, took a left at the end of the aisle, and found myself face-to-face with Nick. He looked as surprised to see me as I was to see him, but his expression quickly changed to one of warning. I glanced over my shoulder. There was a man halfway up the aisle behind me. I didn't know him, but Nick might have.

"Excuse me," I said, squeezing by him.

"Newspaper box outside," he hissed in my ear as I passed. "Watch for me."

I nodded and continued on out the door to the lumberyard. I had to ask for Fred Brookner again, but I finally found him. He was with a customer—Bruno—but he called someone else over to help him while he excused himself to look at the ad.

"No, no, no," he said. "Some of these prices are wrong. Give me a few minutes. I'll get you the right information."

He turned and went inside. I walked back to the door. Nick was just coming out, but he stood aside to let me pass.

"I got the screws you wanted," he called to Bruno. "They're up at the register. You need me to do anything else?"

"Gus should have those parts Larry ordered," he said. "Pick them up and put them in the truck. You can wait for me there. I won't be long."

I was standing at the front counter, waiting for Brookner to correct the prices on the ad, when Nick left the store. I watched him go into the auto parts store across the street and come back carrying a couple of boxes, which he loaded into the back of the pickup truck. Fred Brookner handed me back the ad while I was looking on.

Nick was standing in front of a newspaper dispenser near the truck when I emerged from the hardware store. As soon as he saw me, he dug into his pocket for some change, which he fed into the dispenser. He opened it and pulled out a paper—one of the dailies from the city. Before he closed the dispenser, I saw him slip something in between some of the other papers inside.

"Hey, Nick, what are you up to?" a voice behind me said. Bruno. Had he seen what Nick had done? I spun around to face him.

He broke into a smile, but his eyes skipped back to Nick.

"Just getting a paper," Nick said.

"What do you need a paper for?"

Nick shrugged. "Catch up on what's going on."

"That's what TV is for," Bruno said. He grinned at me. "No offense."

"None taken."

His eyes lingered on me a moment longer. Then, to

Nick: "Come on. We'd better get back."

He pulled his keys from his pocket and headed for the truck.

Nick tucked his newspaper under his arm and climbed up in. I waited until they had driven away before I dug in my own pocket for some change, then opened the dispenser and lifted up one newspaper after another until, finally, there it was, a folded piece of paper. I plucked it out along with a newspaper. It was only as I was closing the box that I realized that someone was watching me: Phil Varton, armored against the sun in his long-sleeved shirt and gloves, spit-polished boots peeking out from under his crisp uniform pants. He peered at me through his mirrored sunglasses. I nodded an acknowledgement, folded my newspaper, and crossed the street to the newspaper office. He was still watching me when I headed inside, wondering how long he had been out there, what, if anything, he had seen, and whether it even mattered.

.   .   .

"I don't think it's a very good idea," Morgan said when I climbed onto the dock after work.

"I don't have a choice. I have to go. He wants to talk to me. What if it's important?"

"He wants to meet you in the middle of nowhere." Morgan nodded at the map that Nick had left for me between newspapers along with a time when he wanted to meet. "Why doesn't he just call you and tell you whatever it is?"

"I don't know. He must have trouble getting to a phone," I said. The only one I had seen at Mr. Wilson's place was in the kitchen. Nick didn't have a cell phone. Bruno hadn't had one with him, either, when he had stopped to help me out of the ditch. Wilson must have had some kind of rule against them. "Or maybe he wants to show me something."

"In the middle of the night in the middle of nowhere? The last time you were out there at night you saw a bear, remember?"

"Nick wouldn't ask me to meet him someplace that wasn't safe."

"Maybe he hasn't heard about that bear."

"You said that that bear was spotted around here. Are you afraid to be here alone, Morgan? Is that it?"

"Of course not," Morgan said stiffly. Then she softened. "Well, maybe a little. But bears have legs, Robyn. They get around. I'm serious. What if you go out there to meet Nick and you run into a bear instead?"

"I'll be in the car," I told her. "And this time I won't drive into the ditch. I'll be fine. I promise."

. . .

Later that night I took the boat across to the marina. I glanced up at Al Duggan's restaurant as I headed for my car. The Closed sign was in the door, but the lights were still on and I saw Duggan inside mopping the floor. Colleen was out behind the restaurant, putting a big garbage bag into the trash. She straightened up when she saw me, but she didn't say anything. I got into my car, checked the map Nick had drawn for me, and pulled out of the lot.

I was fine as long as I was driving. But when I pulled over at what I hoped was the right place and killed the lights, my heart started to flutter. I peered into the woods closest to me. It was too dark. If there was a bear in there, I couldn't see it. I turned to check the woods on the other side of the road, too, just in case—

I heard something crunching over the gravel.

My heart stopped in my chest.

Someone rapped on the window. Nick.

I leaned across the front seat and unlocked the door for him. He climbed in and closed and locked the door behind him.

"I'm almost positive I wasn't followed," he said.

"How did you get here?"

"I walked."

"Through the woods?"

He nodded.

"There are bears around here, Nick."

"Well, I didn't see any. Look, I gotta talk fast. I share a room with this guy—he sleeps like a log. Snores, too, which is why I think I got stuck with him. 'Cause I'm the new guy. But the way it works, if your roommate goes AWOL, you're supposed to tell Larry right away. If you don't and your roommate gets caught, you both get punished. Some guys cover for each other, but I don't know my roommate well enough yet for that. I'm working on it, though."

I still didn't like the idea of him hiking through the woods. "Isn't there a phone somewhere that you can use?" I said, echoing Morgan. "Couldn't you just call me?"

"The only phone is in the house. There's almost always someone around during the day, and at night the house is locked."

Lights flashed in the side-view mirror. Nick grabbed me and pulled me down so that we couldn't be seen by whoever was driving by.

"Why do I feel like you're taking a terrible chance, Nick?"

He smiled. "Because you always feel like that. You worry too much, Robyn." His face grew more serious. "But there's definitely something going on back there."

"What do you mean?"

"The past two nights, guys have left the bunkhouse in the middle of the night."

"Where did they go?"

"I don't know. All I know is that they left after midnight. Not sure when they got back. I tried to stay awake, but it's a lot harder than you'd think, just sitting there in the dark, waiting. I don't know how cops do it—all those stakeouts, I mean."

"You couldn't follow them?"

"I tried the first night. But Derek was out in the yard. I told him I had just wanted to get some air, but . . ." He glanced around again.

"You think he was watching you?"

"I don't know for sure. But I saw him outside the second night, too, so, yeah, maybe."

"What about tonight?"

"Far as I know, I'm the only guy out of the bunkhouse. But it's weird, right? A bunch of guys disappear in the middle of the night and stay gone all night, and Derek's out in the yard, like he's keeping watch?"

It was weird, all right. More lights. Another car. We ducked again.

"I think you should get out of there, Nick."

"Not yet. I have a feeling that something's going to happen. Remember I said I thought they were checking me out?"

I nodded.

"Well, all of a sudden they started asking me a lot of questions."

"What kind of questions?"

"Mostly personal stuff—about my family, my past, what I did, things like that. But mostly about my family and who I know back in the city."

"What did you tell them?"

"That I'm on my own. That I've been trying to get it together since I got out of custody. That kind of stuff."

"I talked to my dad's friend," I said.

Nick did not look pleased. "I said no cops. I don't

want anyone saying anything to Larry about me. Especially not now. I'm telling you, Robyn. They're up to something. What if that's the reason Lucas wants to get out of there? What if Alex felt the same way? I have to find out what happened to him. I promised Seth."

"I know. And I didn't mention you to Chief Lafayette. I'm working on that article for the paper, remember? When I talked to him, it was for the article. Nick, he's positive Alex's death was suicide."

Nick seemed reluctant to believe it.

"Did Lucas say anything about a kid named Steven?" I said.

"Steven? No. Why?"

"There was a kid named Steven who took off last winter."

"I heard about two other guys who took off," Nick said. "But neither of them was named Steven. What's his story?"

"His story is that he's dead," I said. "I was wondering if he's the guy Lucas told you about. He said there was someone besides Alex who died, right?"

Nick nodded. "But he didn't tell me his name."

I filled him in on what Colleen had told me and what I had learned from Mr. Kastner at the record store.

"It sounds like you were right, Nick. Lucas knew that Mr. Kastner was watching him, but he shoplifted anyway. Kastner said that usually when kids steal, they're not so obvious about it and that they come in groups and one of them distracts him. But the boy who was with Lucas didn't try to distract Kastner. He didn't seem to know what was going on. The way Lucas acted was just plain stupid—unless he wanted to get caught. And that kid Steven? He definitely wanted to get away from Larry Wilson's, even though the only place he had to go was his foster home. Whatever happened to them at Wilson's, the two of them were desperate to get out of there. It doesn't sound safe, Nick. I think you should leave too."

Nick shook his head. He could be so stubborn.

"Alex told Seth he wanted to leave," he said. "Maybe he was scared like Lucas is. Maybe someone threatened him. Maybe walking into the lake was the only way he could figure to deal with it. And maybe they're asking me all these questions for a reason—hoping to get me involved in whatever goes on there at night. I have to find out."

"You said Lucas sounded scared. What if there's a good reason for that, Nick? What if he—"

"I'll be careful, Robyn, I promise. And don't worry—I'm not going to run away, and I'm sure not going to kill myself. Why would I do something like that when I have you out here waiting for me?" He pulled me close to him. "Meet me back here on Friday night, okay? Same time."

"What if you can't get away?"

"Wait half an hour. If I don't show up, I'll figure out some other way to contact you."

I didn't like the sound of it.

"Those other two guys who ran away—do you know their names, Nick?"

"Yeah. Why?"

"Maybe I could look into it."

"How? You're not going to talk to that cop again, are you, Robyn?"

"I was thinking maybe Ed Jarvis." Nick's probation contact. "He might be able to tell me something about those kids. I can tell him the same thing I told my dad's friend: I'm doing a story for the paper. It's not like it's a lie."

"Okay," Nick said. "But background only. No details. And don't mention me, okay?"

"Okay."

He told me the names of the two boys who had run away.

"Friday night, Robyn."

He kissed me, reached for the door handle, kissed me again, and then got out of the car and disappeared into the night.

I turned the car around and headed back to town. I hadn't gone more than a couple of miles before another car appeared in my rearview mirror. At first it was several car lengths behind me, but the gap soon closed so that all I could see in my side view was the glare of the car's headlights. I started to get nervous. There was no oncoming traffic and the road was wide enough for passing, but the car was tailgating me.

I checked the rearview mirror again. All I could see

was a shadowy figure behind the wheel. I increased my speed a little. The car stayed with me.

I told myself not to panic. If the car was still following me by the time I got back to town, I would pull over at the first gas station, restaurant, or fast-food place that I came to and call Dean Lafayette.

Suddenly the car fell back a little. Then it pulled out into the middle of the road and picked up speed again. I felt myself go cold all over as the car drew parallel with me. I glanced over at the driver. It took me a few seconds—I had never seen him without his mirrored sunglasses on. Phil Varton. He looked at me for a moment, then pulled ahead of me.

Get a grip, Robyn, I told myself. *He's a cop. He's supposed to be one of the good guys.*

But Nick didn't share that opinion. He'd seen Varton talking to Larry a couple of times. Varton had also been in charge of investigating Alex Richmond's death.

His taillights got smaller and then disappeared when his car rounded a bend. When I reached the same bend, the road ahead was deserted. I didn't see another car until I reached town. But when I finally got to the marina parking lot and pulled the key out of the ignition, my hands were shaking.

CHAPTER TWELVE

I called Ed Jarvis from my cell phone the next day during my lunch break. He wasn't in his office, so I left him a message. He didn't return my call until I got back to Morgan's summerhouse that evening. I told him about the article I was writing and gave him the two names that Nick had given me.

"I don't recognize those names," Ed said. "And even if I did, I'm not sure what I could tell you. Anything in their files is probably confidential—to anyone, especially to the press, which, in this case, you are."

"I don't want to know about what kind of trouble they were in," I said. "That's not what my story is about. I was just wondering if you could find out where they are now or what happened to them after they left Larry Wilson's place. If I can track them down, maybe they would agree to talk to me."

I heard a chuckle at the other end of the phone.

"Your dad was the most tenacious cop I ever met," he said. "Your mother has developed a reputation as a tenacious lawyer. And now you—a tenacious reporter."

"I'm not really a reporter," I said. "It's just a summer job, and I'm only working on this story because it's something I care about."

"Ah, passion," he said. "The perfect partner to tenacity. Okay, I'll see what I can find out. But it could take a few days. And there's no guarantee that I'll find anything or that I'll be able to tell you what I do find."

. . .

Ed Jarvis didn't call the next day or the day after that. Mr. Hartford sent me out to cover the annual summer walk-a-thon, so that kept me busy for a while. But by Friday I could barely concentrate on what I was doing. I hadn't seen any of Larry's kids in town on errands for days. I was worried about Nick. And I was anxious for Ed Jarvis to call back.

Finally, after supper on Friday, my phone rang.

"I hate to tell you this, Robyn," Ed Jarvis said, "but I don't think I'm going to be too helpful. I checked both those names you gave me. Both files list Larry Wilson's group home as their last known address. Wilson reported that they had left his group home, but there's nothing in either file that indicates where they went after that. There's no record of either of them returning to the city. They could be anywhere."

"What about their families? Do you think they might know where either of them are?"

"They don't have families."

"Neither of them?"

"Nope. Both started in foster care at a young age. Neither got adopted. And both got caught up in the system early on. That's pretty much all I can tell you."

"Well, thanks anyway," I said.

"Bad news?" Morgan said when I closed my phone.

"Worse," I said. "No news."

. . .

"You're not seriously going out there again tonight?" Morgan said.

"I told Nick I would."

"Don't you think you should talk to that cop friend of your dad's?"

"I promised Nick I wouldn't. Not yet, anyway."

"But—"

"The minute I think there's any serious danger, I'll call my dad. But so far nothing has happened. I don't even know if anything will happen."

I reviewed everything I knew about Larry Wilson's kids.

Lucas wasn't happy at Larry Wilson's place. And according to Nick, he was ready to do just about anything to get away from there.

Steven had been unhappy there too—so unhappy

that he'd been willing to return to foster parents who didn't want him. When that wasn't possible, he ran away, got lost in the woods, and died.

Alex Richmond had also wanted to leave Wilson's place. He had been found drowned in the lake out there.

A couple of other boys had run away—so far away that no one knew where they were.

But what did that prove? Did it prove anything?

All four boys had been in trouble with the law. And one thing I had learned about kids like the ones at Wilson's place was that they didn't always deal with their problems in a rational way. Lucas had tried to solve his problem by stealing. Steven had anger-management issues—maybe the cracked window at the marina restaurant hadn't been his fault, but he had broken the phone.

But—and it was a big but—Nick was convinced that something was going on out there. Something that happened late at night. Something that involved Derek standing watch in the compound. Something that might involve Phil Varton, the cop who had investigated Alex Richmond's death. Was it possible that he'd covered up the real cause? As long as Nick was out there, I had to do whatever I could to make sure he was okay.

"I'm going to meet Nick. It'll be fine. I'll have my phone with me. You'll be the second person I call if anything happens."

"Second?"

"First I'll call Dean Lafayette."

$\cdot \quad \cdot \quad \cdot$

I drove to the same place I had met Nick earlier in the week. I sat at the side of the road, peering into the darkened woods.

I waited for half an hour.

I waited for forty-five minutes.

I waited for an hour.

Nick didn't show.

$\cdot \quad \cdot \quad \cdot$

"Maybe that roommate of his had trouble sleeping, so Nick couldn't get away," Morgan said. "Or maybe he got caught sneaking out. You said yourself that Mr. Wilson is really strict with the kids."

"Maybe." I knew that what she was saying made sense. What had Larry Wilson told me? That he expected them to play by the rules. "You're probably right," I said.

$\cdot \quad \cdot \quad \cdot$

By Sunday I still hadn't heard from Nick. He hadn't made it back to Morgan's place. He hadn't shown up in town—and I had spent all day Saturday prowling around, hoping that he'd come in on an errand. He didn't call, either. I turned to Morgan, who was dozing on a lounge chair next to me on the veranda. I didn't want to admit it to her, but I was worried.

"Come on," I said. "Get dressed." I grabbed her crutches, which were leaning against the veranda railing, and handed them to her.

She yawned and stirred lazily. "I was having such a nice dream."

"You sleep too much." She had come outside in her bathing suit, stretched out on a lounge chair in the mid-morning heat, and promptly fallen asleep again while I sat staring out at the water and fretting about Nick.

"What else is there to do? I'm bored. Try having a cast on your leg, see how energetic you feel."

"That's why you have to get dressed. We're going into town."

"What for?" she said. "There's nothing to do there, either. It's as boring there as it is here. I used to love coming up here every summer. Now I'd rather be back home."

"That charity baseball game is happening this afternoon—the fire department against Mr. Wilson's kids," I said. "Maybe Nick will be there." If he wasn't, I would be more than worried.

"And Bruno will be playing for Larry's team. I bet Derek will be too."

She sat up. "Well," she said slowly, "now that I'm wide awake, I guess I might as well go. It doesn't matter how great a dream is—and the one I was having was amazing—you can't make it happen again. Once it's gone, it's gone." She reached for her crutches and struggled to her feet.

"Don't be such a grouch," I said. "Maybe you'll be pleasantly surprised. Maybe one of those volunteer firefighters will turn out to be the man of your dreams."

. . .

Nick wasn't at the park where the game was being held.

I saw Bruno. I saw Derek. I saw Lucas. I saw all of the other guys who had been around the table the night I'd had supper at Larry's place. They were all sitting on a bench to one side of the backstop, wearing yellow T-shirts that said *Larry's Kids* on the back. Mr. Wilson, also in a yellow T-shirt, was talking to the umpire.

The volunteer firefighters in their red T-shirts had congregated on the other side of the backstop. A large crowd had gathered. The bleachers were almost full.

But I didn't see Nick anywhere.

"The only empty seats I see are way up there," Morgan said in a peevish voice. She pointed to the upper level of the bleachers. "If I start climbing now, I might make it up there by the end of the seventh inning."

"Stay here," I said. "I'll talk to the organizers. Maybe they can do something for you."

I left her where she was and doubled back around the bleachers to where the ticket-sellers and ticket-takers were.

A bright yellow T-shirt was coming toward me.

Nick.

Thank god.

He didn't even look at me as he walked past. I glanced around, confused, and saw Phil Varton watching Nick through his mirrored sunglasses.

The important thing, I told myself, was that Nick was here and he was okay.

One of the ticket-takers referred me to a woman who was selling tickets, who referred me to a man who turned out to be the event organizer—and the recently retired chief of the volunteer fire department.

"No problem," he said. "Give me a sec. We'll set you up."

A few minutes later he carried two folding chairs over to where Morgan and I were waiting and set them up a couple of feet from the bench occupied by Larry's kids. Morgan cheered up considerably and started making eyes at Derek. And at Bruno.

"Which one do you think is hotter, Robyn? Derek has great eyes, but that tattoo, I don't know, it's kind of clichéd, don't you think? Bruno's eyes are kind of muddy-colored and nondescript. But he has great hair. And amazing teeth, considering."

"Considering?"

"Most of those guys come from messed-up families. Call it stereotyping, but I don't associate great dental care with messed-up families."

The teams were introduced. A roar went up when the mayor read out the fire department lineup. People stamped their feet and whistled for every player. It was a different story when the mayor read the lineup for Larry's team. A couple of Larry's kids turned and scowled at the crowd. Most just stared stonily ahead and pretended that they hadn't heard the scattered heckling or didn't care. I glanced at Nick. He said something to Bruno, who was sitting beside him. Bruno shrugged. He'd been at Larry's place the longest. I guess he was used to it.

The firefighters were good. They scored one run in the first inning, another run in the third inning, and kept their lead—for a while. The crowd cheered whenever they got a base hit or sent someone home—and every time one of Larry's kids struck out.

"It's root, root, root for the home team, big time," Morgan said, glancing around.

The firefighters were strutting confidently by the time the seventh-inning stretch rolled around. They sent another man home. The score was three to one.

At the bottom of the ninth, the crowd started to jeer Larry's kids.

"Give it up."

"You're done."

"Losers."

Wilson looked at the guys on his bench. He nodded at Lucas, who was next at bat.

Lucas struck out.

The crowd roared.

Tal was up next.

He struck out.

The crowd roared.

Then Nick was up. His face was tense and strained.

He swung—and missed.

The crowd went crazy, cheering and booing at the same time.

The pitcher wound up again.

Nick swung . . .

. . . and made contact.

He dropped the bat and ran. He got to first base a split second before the ball did. The crowd was silent.

Another of Larry's kids went up and got two strikes. Then he made a base hit. Nick ran to second.

The crowd was silent.

Derek was up next. He hit the first ball to come his way—another base hit. Now the bases were loaded.

The crowd started to boo, but the guys on Larry's bench were smiling.

Larry nodded to Bruno, who stepped up to the plate.

He swung—and missed. Strike one.

He swung again—and missed again. Strike two.

Morgan reached over and squeezed my hand.

The pitcher looked at the catcher and wound up again. The ball shot through the air.

Bruno swung—crack! The ball sailed through the air—high, fast, far.

Nick sprinted for home. I sprang to my feet, cheering. Morgan whistled.

The next kid came home.

Larry's kids roared.

Derek came home.

Larry's kids were on their feet, stomping and clapping. The ball had hit the ground somewhere in the distance, and guys in the outfield were chasing it. But it was too late. Bruno bounded in to home plate. The score was 4–3. Larry's kids had won in a major upset. They were jumping up and down.

A couple of Larry's kids turned to look at the firefighters. I saw contempt and anger in some firefighter faces. Then one firefighter said something. I didn't catch the words, but I didn't have to hear them to know that it was no compliment. Nick lunged at the guy. Before Larry Wilson could get to him and pull him off, Derek, Bruno, and some of the others went to his rescue. Or maybe they just went to work off their own resentment. The umpire, the mayor, Dean Lafayette, Phil Varton, and Wilson had their work cut out for them separating the combatants. Morgan scrambled precariously on her crutches to avoid getting hurt. Someone grabbed me. I spun around. It was Nick. He thrust something into my hand and then darted away.

CHAPTER **THIRTEEN**

"I don't care what you say," Morgan said the next day after I got home from work. "This time I'm going with you."

"Okay," I said.

"I mean it, Robyn. I'm tired of sitting around here while you have all the excitement. Besides—"

"I said okay, Morgan."

She eyed me suspiciously. "You're trying to trick me into believing you. Then you're going to run to the dock, jump in the boat, and speed away before I can react. Right?"

"Wrong."

Her suspicion deepened. "You're actually going to let me go with you?"

"I was just about to ask you if you would."

"Uh huh."

"Really. I was."

She peered at me. "What's the catch, Robyn?"

"Every time Nick leaves the compound, there's someone with him. Usually it's one of the older guys—Bruno or Derek. So, assuming this actually works, I need you there to keep whoever's with him occupied while Nick tells me whatever it is he wants to tell me. You think you can do that?"

"Do I think I can distract a guy for a couple of minutes? Please! Just let me get changed."

"There's no time."

"You're not going like that, are you?"

I looked down at my blue T-shirt and white capris.

"What's wrong with what I'm wearing?"

"Well, nothing, I guess. But if you expect me to distract anyone, you're going to have to give me five minutes."

"No."

"Two?"

"We have to go now, Morgan, or we'll be late."

She pouted. Then she crutched her way into the house double-time.

"Morgan!"

She was back a moment later with a tote bag over one shoulder. "I'll change in the car."

. . .

By the time we got to the spot Nick had indicated on his map, Morgan was attired in a scarlet top and a floaty, multicolored skirt. But she was frowning.

"What's the matter? You look great," I said.

"This stupid cast really ruins the look. It ruins all my looks."

"I'm sure you'll do fine." I opened the car door and circled around to the rear passenger wheel. Then I pulled out the tool that Nick had told me to buy, and, following the little diagram he had drawn, deflated the tire. I opened the trunk, wrestled out the spare, pulled out the jack, and removed the tire iron. I leaned the tire against the back of the car, stood the jack beside it, and hid the tire iron in a bag I had brought along. I stashed the bag on the floor of the car under the front seat.

"Now what?" Morgan said.

"Now we wait."

"What if someone comes along before Nick does and insists on helping us?"

"We act all insulted and tell them that just because we're girls, that doesn't mean we don't know how to change a tire."

Morgan nodded. She thought for a moment.

"What if no one shows up?"

"Then we change the tire."

"Meaning you wrestle that filthy flat tire off and put the disgusting spare one on," Morgan said. "I told you that you should have changed, Robyn."

I looked down at my crisp white capris. I hate it when Morgan is right.

.   .   .

"Now," Morgan said. She was standing beside the car, leaning on her crutches and looking fetchingly helpless. I was poised for action. At her cue, I picked up the jack and carried it to the deflated tire.

"They're slowing down," Morgan said.

A black pickup truck drove slowly past the car and parked in front of it. Derek jumped down from the driver's side door.

"Problem, ladies?"

"I have it under control," I said.

Morgan looked at me, surprised. "I thought—"

I elbowed her into silence.

Derek circled around to look at the flat tire. He looked at the jack. Then he looked into the open trunk.

"Where's your tire iron?"

"My what?"

Morgan put a hand over her mouth to hide a smile.

Derek shook his head. "Hey, Nick," he called. "Get over here. Bring the tire iron."

A moment later the pickup's passenger door opened and Nick climbed out. He circled to the back of the truck, fiddled with the storage compartment behind the cab, and jumped down from the truck bed with a tire iron in his hand. He loped over to where Derek and I were standing and started to position the jack.

"My ankle's killing me," Morgan said. "I'm going to wait in the car."

"We have to jack it up," Derek said. "If you want to sit down, go and sit in the truck."

Morgan looked doubtfully at the pickup. "I don't think I can get up there by myself," she said. "Not on crutches."

I wanted to hug her. Her performance was perfect.

Nick finished jacking up the car and reached for the tire iron.

"Why don't you give her a hand?" he said, winking slyly at Derek. "I'll stay here and take care of this."

"Yeah, okay." Derek walked over to Morgan and asked her if she needed any help. She said no, she was fine and then—this is why I really love Morgan—she stumbled, gave a little yelp, and started to fall. Derek grabbed her around the waist and held her up. One of her crutches clattered to the ground. Derek leaned her gently against the car and retrieved it for her.

"Are you okay?" he said as he handed the crutch to Morgan. She said she was, but all of a sudden she had a lot more trouble moving her crutches. Derek walked beside her, ready to catch her if she stumbled again. He opened the passenger door and helped her up into the truck. I watched, holding my breath. Derek looked back at Nick, who was removing another lug nut. He circled around the truck and climbed in behind the wheel. I started to move closer to Nick.

"Stay where you are," Nick said. "That way Derek can see you. Look around. Act like you're just waiting for me to get the job done, okay? Don't talk to me."

I started to nod, but caught myself. I realized why Nick had asked me to deflate that specific tire. It was the one farthest from the pickup. He was almost completely out of Derek's sight line while he worked on it.

"I overheard Larry and Derek talking about the old sawmill. But they were all mysterious about it."

I kept my back to the truck and my voice low. "Larry told me he'd suggested that the county turn it into a museum."

"I don't think that's what they were talking about," Nick said. "It was almost like they were speaking in code. Maybe it has something to do with what happened to Alex. Plus, Bruno's been asking me a lot of questions. Larry, too. I get the feeling he's starting to trust me. He keeps asking me if the opportunity came up to make a little money, would I be interested, even if it was hard work. I told him, yeah, sure. And Bruno has been asking more about my family, my record, stuff like that. They're keeping an eye on me, for sure."

"Do you want me to talk to my dad's friend?"

"And tell him what? That one of Larry's kids thinks something is going on out there? I have no idea what it is, so how is he going to figure it out? Hey, Robyn, can you come back here and give me a hand?"

I walked back to where he was crouched and helped him roll the old tire away from the car.

"You said it has something to do with the sawmill. Maybe he could check it out."

"How's he going to do that? Ask Larry? If there really is something going on, Larry isn't going to tell him."

"He could search the property," I said. Nick hoisted

the spare tire from the trunk and dropped it onto the gravel. I glanced at the truck and saw Derek twist around to see how Nick was doing.

"Five minutes," Nick called, holding up five fingers. Derek nodded. Nick rolled the spare over to the rear wheel well and squatted down to fit it into place.

"Your dad was a cop. Your mom's a lawyer, so you should know better. The sawmill is on private property. The cops can't search it without either permission from Larry or a search warrant. And they can't get a warrant without probable cause, which they don't have because I have no idea what's happening. And if there really is something going on, Larry would let them look around. Anyway, if they ask, Larry will know someone said something. He's beginning to trust me, Robyn. I don't want to blow that."

"Okay," I said. "Then how about if I check out the sawmill and see if I can find out what's going on?"

"I don't know. If I'm right, it could be dangerous."

"You said those guys left the bunkhouse at night. I'll check it out during the day."

"I don't know—"

I heard the truck door open. Derek jumped out.

"Nick, you done or what?"

"Yeah," Nick said. He tightened the last nut and jacked the car down. He threw the jack into the trunk and wrestled the flat tire in after it. Then he slammed the trunk lid down while Derek helped Morgan down from the cab of the truck.

"You should get that tire fixed right away," Nick said, his voice loud enough for Derek to hear. "You don't want to be out driving around without a spare."

"Okay," I said.

"I mean it. Right away."

I nodded. Nick picked up the tire iron and headed back to the truck.

"Drive carefully, ladies," Derek said. "I'm not always going to be around to bail you out, you know."

I thanked him. Morgan waved cheerily at him. We got back in the car, and I started the engine. Derek and Nick climbed into the pickup and drove away.

"Remind me never to get into a truck with that guy again," Morgan said.

"Did he try anything?"

"No. But there's something about him—he gives me the creeps."

I put the car into gear, and we started back to town. While I drove, I filled Morgan in on what Nick had told me.

"What are you going to do?" she said.

"I'm going to ask Mr. Hartford if he'll give me tomorrow afternoon off."

.   .   .

"This is crazy," Morgan said the next afternoon as I packed her camera into my backpack. "You're crazy. What if someone sees you?"

"Sees me do what? I'm just going for a hike. I'm going to take a few pictures of that old church."

Mr. Hartford had given me the afternoon off to work on my story. Before I had left the newspaper office, I'd chatted with Margie Harris upstairs about the history of the area, particularly its early days as a logging site. She mentioned an old church a few miles north of the old logging camp and the sawmill on Larry Wilson's property.

"It's on private property, so you would have to get permission," she said. "But if you hike a few miles north, there's a lovely old church that used to operate during the logging season. There's a cemetery there, too . . ."

She'd unfolded a map of the area and showed me where to find the church.

"Besides," I said to Morgan as I tucked the map into my pocket, "if Nick is right, whatever is going on out there goes on at night. I'm going during the day."

"When you'll be easier to spot," Morgan pointed out.

"When normal people go hiking." My dad had told me one time that if you act suspiciously, you'll make people suspicious. The trick is to look normal. "Or would you rather I go out there after dark?"

Morgan shuddered and shook her head.

"Don't you think you should at least talk to your dad?"

I did. And I had tried. But either something was wrong with his cell phone, or something was wrong with the signal way over there on the other side of the world.

"I can't get through to him," I said.

"What about your mom?"

"You're kidding, right? What do you think my mom would say if she knew Nick was up here, never mind if I told her what I'm about to do?"

"Right," Morgan said. She knew how my mom felt about Nick. She also knew that my mom would freak out if I even started to tell her about my plan.

"It shouldn't take long," I said. "I'll have my phone on vibrate, just in case. I'll call you when I'm on my way home."

.   .   .

Even though I had told Morgan not to worry, my heart was racing as I turned onto a narrow road just east of Wild River Road. I parked beside some bushes so that my car wouldn't immediately be seen by anyone who happened to drive by.

It was a warm, bright day. I hiked from where I had parked the car to the banks of the Wild River, which was more like a stream and looked about as wild as the average house cat, and followed it south until I came to a chain-link fence. From there I hiked west until I came to a gate. The fence was high and sturdy and new. Its gate had a sign attached: Private Property. No Trespassing. A rusted padlock held it shut.

I continued along the fence for a few feet but didn't

see any gaps. I doubled back to the gate, looked around in all directions, and then grabbed the chain-link, shoving the toes of my hiking boots into the openings. Once I'd climbed to the top, I swung my legs over and dropped down to the other side. I stood there for a moment, breathing hard, and wondered how fast I could climb back over if I had to.

I told myself to relax. I had been careful. No one had seen me. Besides, it was daylight. I checked my map again. I was on the logging road. Wilson had been right about it—it was in terrible shape. In some places it was all washboardy. In others, chunks of road were missing altogether. I had trouble imagining that it was used anymore. I thought about that rusty old lock and wondered how long it had been since anyone had unlocked it.

I decided to get off the road and walk in the woods, where I would be less visible. That's when I noticed wheel ruts several feet away from the logging road, running roughly parallel to it. Vehicle traffic of some kind had cut deeply into the shrubs, and from the look of it, that traffic had been repeated and relatively recent.

I stayed among the trees and peered around, but I didn't see anything. I kept walking until I finally spotted a building in a clearing up ahead. The old sawmill.

It stood in a weedy clearing, but there were tire tracks in the gravel and dirt around it. Wide and deep, same as the ones near the old logging road. *A truck must have made them*, I thought.

The sawmill was a large, squat building. Part of it

was open on one side and filled with rusty old equipment, piles old lumber, and a series of covered wooden bins. I crept inside and looked around. I even opened the bins. Most of them were empty. One was filled with pieces of scrap wood.

The rest of the sawmill was closed in. I circled around until I found a door. Locked.

Tall, grimy windows ran all around the enclosed section. I went up on tiptoes and peeked in. There was more equipment inside, but it was hard to make out through the dirt just what it was. I tried to open the window above me. It was locked. I tried the next one. It was also locked. I circled the building, trying window after window. Locked, locked, locked . . .

The last window moved when I pushed up on it.

I went up on my tiptoes and pushed it higher. Then I grabbed the sill and pulled myself up so I could look inside.

The contents of this building were newer than those of the adjacent saw shed. Much newer.

The large, open room was filled with car parts— fenders, bumpers, tires, wheel assemblies, all stacked in neat piles. Well, Larry Wilson had said he stripped down junked cars and sold whatever he could. He was also teaching the boys auto repair, and I knew that he bought parts from an automotive store in town.

But this was a lot of stuff, and even though I didn't know much about cars, it didn't look like parts from clunkers.

I dropped back down to the ground and swung my backpack around. I took out Morgan's camera, wrapped the strap around my wrist, and pulled myself up again. This time I swung a leg up over the sill and dropped down inside.

Morgan would have had a fit if she'd seen me. She would have said, I suppose if you heard weird sounds coming from your basement in the middle of the night, you wouldn't call the police. No, you'd be like those idiots in horror movies and decide to go investigate. You know what happens to those people, right, Robyn?

Yeah, I knew.

But this was different. This was the middle of the day, and there wasn't a soul around.

I went over to a stack of fenders and took a picture. I took a dozen pictures of all the parts.

A small table stood at the back of the room, covered with car specs and tools. I slid open a drawer in the table and found a small metal box inside. It was filled with little metal rectangles that had numbers stamped into them. I was pretty sure I knew what they were. I was right. It meant Nick had been right, too. I took a picture of the box and slipped one of the metal rectangles into the pocket in my backpack where I kept my notebook. I was about to zip it up again when I heard something.

A crunching sound . . . like car tires on gravel.

A car door slammed.

I ran to the open window, threw my backpack out, and crawled out over the sill. My heart was pounding as I dropped to the hard earth below. For a moment I crouched there, paralyzed. Then I looked up.

The window. It was still open.

I stood up and cautiously peeked inside. The door on the other side of the room was opening, and I saw a gloved hand slip inside. I yanked the window shut and ducked down out of sight. Shouldering my backpack, I crept along the side of the building, staying low. I had planned to dash for the cover of the woods, but I heard a sound that sent a chill up my spine. Another car was approaching. I dared a glace around the side of the building. Not a car—a Jeep. I ducked back around the building. Above me, a window slid open.

"Open another one," a familiar voice said. Derek. "Jeez, it's hot in here."

Another window opened. I went down to my hands and knees and crept away from it as fast as I could. I looked out at the woods beyond the clearing. If I could get there, I could creep away unseen. But what if someone was looking out one of the windows?

I heard another sound. This one was louder and deeper, getting closer and closer. A truck.

Whatever was happening at the sawmill, it wasn't happening only at night.

I glanced back over my shoulder. Where to go? Where to run?

The Jeep was parked in front of the building. The truck had cut off the far end of the building and any escape from the rear. It was enormous, with a huge container, like a shipping container, behind the massive cab.

I darted around to the open-sided part of the building. That's when I caught a glimpse of the first car that had arrived. A police car.

Police car. Gloved hand.

Phil Varton.

"Put that over here," another voice said. I recognized it instantly—Larry Wilson. I heard footsteps crunching over gravel. They were coming toward me.

I ducked inside the open building and looked around wildly.

"Come on, come on," Wilson said impatiently.

I darted behind a pile of old lumber and crouched down out of sight.

Bad move.

I was trapped. Something—from the sound of it, something big—was being unloaded right in front of the open-sided building where I was hiding.

"Line them up here," Mr. Wilson said. "We'll take care of them tonight."

Tonight?

How long was I going to have to stay here?

I thought about the phone in my backpack. If I could get it out, I could text Morgan and tell her what was happening.

"We should clear all of this lumber out," Derek said. "We'd have more room."

I heard footsteps coming toward me. Two gloved

hands appeared right above me, coming down to grab some of the lumber that was shielding me from view.

No, no.

I couldn't take my eyes off the gloved hands. There was a big grease stain on the right index finger. They looked larger than life as they closed around a piece of lumber and started to lift it.

"We don't have time for that," Mr. Wilson said. "We have to load up all the stuff from inside. We can take care of that another time."

I breathed a silent sigh of relief, but I didn't dare try to wriggle out of my backpack so that I could contact Morgan. I crouched motionless behind the lumber while people worked around me. Time seemed to be both speeding and crawling by at the same time. I was terrified I would be discovered. I kept checking my watch. An hour passed. Then another.

Something vibrated against my back—my phone. Morgan? A little later it vibrated again.

"Okay," Mr. Wilson said at last. "That's it for now. I'll send some of the guys out here later. We'll get busy tonight, and tomorrow night we'll be ready to roll. By the end of the week these'll be halfway around the world."

A car door slammed and an engine turned over. Then I heard another engine—the Jeep. It drove away. But I didn't hear the truck rev up.

I stayed hidden where I was. My legs were cramped. My stomach was rumbling. After an hour of complete silence, I decided to chance a peek.

I crept out from behind the pile of lumber. Four luxury cars now stood in the open-sided building where I had been hiding.

I headed out the way I had come. The truck was still parked along the far end of the building, but I didn't see or hear anyone. Maybe whoever had been in the truck had gone with the Jeep. I waited, my heart pounding in my chest. The only thing I heard was birdsong. I decided to take my chances.

First I crept over to the cars. They looked new. I opened one of the doors and sniffed inside. The car appeared to be in mint condition, but it didn't have that new-car smell. Instead, I caught a hint of perfume, tinged with the sour scent of sweat. Almost-brand-new car, no new-car smell. Not good. I checked the rest of the cars, snapped pictures of them, and then made my way back to the fence as fast as I could.

The gate was locked. I looked around. No one in sight. On rubbery legs I climbed up and over the fence and started back to my car, sticking to the woods on one side of the road in case anyone decided to return to the sawmill.

I was close to my destination when I heard a loud snap that brought me to a halt. Was I being followed?

I heard another snap, louder, closer. Someone was definitely out there. A form lumbered into view.

I tried to stay calm, but panic got the better of me, and I let out a strangled scream.

CHAPTER **FOURTEEN**

*T*hink, I told myself. *Remember what Morgan told you.* But I couldn't think, and I couldn't remember. The bear blocking my path looked like a gigantic, furry boulder. It wasn't moving. It was too busy staring at me.

My first instinct was to look away. I knew that if you stared a strange dog in the eyes, it was likely to take it as a challenge. I didn't know if the same was true for bears, but I wasn't going to take any chances. I stood as still as a tree.

Wave your arms—I was pretty sure Morgan had said you were supposed to do that. It made you look bigger. I peeked at the bear. It hadn't budged. I wasn't sure if that was a good thing or a bad thing—maybe it was getting ready to pounce. What if waving my arms startled it?

Make noise, Morgan had also said. That would scare off bears that weren't used to people. But what did it do to bears who were used to people and who weren't frightened of them?

I couldn't think of anything else to do. I threw my arms up and yelled, "Yah! Yah!"

The bear reared up on its hind legs, then dropped back down onto all fours. I couldn't breathe. I felt like I was going to faint.

"Back away," said a calm voice behind me.

My legs refused to move.

"Back away slowly. Don't be scared. I've got a gun."

I forced my leaden legs to take a stumbling step backward. The bear stayed where it was. I managed another step, then a third.

The bear tilted its head to one side and watched me. I stepped back again and caught my foot on something—a tree root, I think. I fell backwards to the ground.

The bear turned and bolted through the woods. Two hands grabbed my shoulders and hauled me to my feet.

"Are you all right?"

I wasn't. I was shaking all over, and my back was throbbing. I had fallen hard right onto my backpack, and the camera inside had slammed into my back. I prayed that I hadn't broken it. I wanted to check but hesitated— my rescuer was Phil Varton.

What was he doing here? Had he seen me at the sawmill? Had he followed me? As usual, his eyes were hidden behind mirrored sunglasses, but for once he was gloveless. I stared at his hands. The skin on them was red and purple and shiny. It looked like they had both been badly burned at some point. I wondered if his arms had been burned as well. That would account for the long-sleeved shirts he always wore.

"I've been looking for you," he said. "Your friend called the chief. She said you were hiking out here and she couldn't get hold of you. She was worried, what with the reports of bears and all. The chief sent me out to check on you."

I fumbled in my pocket for my phone. "I must have shut it off by accident," I said. "I'll call her."

"A city girl like you should be careful out in the woods. Bears aren't the only hazard around here."

I had to fight to hide what I was feeling. I was sure he was trying to intimidate me.

"I'm just heading to town now," I said. "I'll call my friend and tell her I'm okay."

"What were you doing out here all alone anyway?"

"Seeing the sights. There's an old church not far from here."

I couldn't see his eyes, so it was impossible to tell if he believed me.

"Come on," he said finally. "Let's get you back to your car."

He held my arm for a few paces, until I told him I was fine and could manage on my own. He shrugged, let go, and led the way. Five minutes later I was at my car.

"You're sure you're going to be okay?" he said.

I nodded. "Thanks for your help. I'm going straight back to town. And staying there."

He looked at me for another moment before turning

and walking down the road to wherever he had parked his patrol car.

I unlocked my car, dug Morgan's camera out of the backpack, and tossed the backpack onto the passenger seat. I whispered a silent prayer as I pressed the camera's ON button. A green light blinked at me. *Thank you, thank you, thank you!*

I scrolled through the pictures I had taken. They were all there. What a relief! I was shutting it off when someone said, "Did you get some good ones?"

I was so startled that I almost dropped the camera.

A police car had pulled up alongside my car—Phil Varton's police car.

"Excuse me?" I said.

"Pictures," he said, nodding at the camera. "Did you get some good pictures?"

"A few. But I don't know how good they are." Before he could ask me if he could see them, I said, "I'd better get back. Thanks for checking on me. And for helping me with the bear."

I climbed into my car and sat there, shaken, hoping he would drive away. But he didn't. He waited for me to make a move. I started my engine, put the camera in the glove compartment, and pulled out onto the gravel road. While I drove back to town, I called Morgan.

"Robyn!" she said breathlessly. "Thank God. I've been calling and calling. I was worried."

I glanced in the rearview mirror. Phil Varton was right behind me. "Morgan, did you call the police?"

"I'm sorry. Don't be mad at me, Robyn. But I really was getting worried. I called the station, and they said they'd send someone to look for you."

"It's okay," I said. Whatever else Phil Varton had been doing out here, he had been telling the truth about being asked to look for me. Dean Lafayette must have radioed him. If only he knew how close he'd come to finding me earlier.

"Did you learn anything, Robyn? Did you—"

I checked the rearview mirror again. Phil Varton was still following me, and I felt myself trembling all over. I had been terrified back at the sawmill and again facing that bear. All I wanted was to get safely back to town.

"I'll call you as soon as I get to the marina, Morgan. I promise."

I took a deep breath and forced myself to concentrate on my driving. Phil Varton stayed with me until I got to the marina parking lot. Then he turned and parked across the street in front of the police station. I grabbed my backpack, locked the car, and walked down to the water to call Morgan again.

"I'm at the marina," I said.

"I know. I can see you. I'm out on the dock with binoculars. Are you okay?"

"Apart from almost being attacked by a bear?"

"A bear!?"

I glanced around. There were some people nearby, so I walked out onto the dock where I would have some privacy and told her what I had found out in the woods.

"And stumbling on a car-theft ring," I said.

"Car-theft ring? Out at Mr. Wilson's place?"

"Yeah."

"Are you sure?"

"There are a lot of car parts stashed out there. And they didn't look like they had come direct from the factory, either." Next I told her about the little box of numbered metal plates I had discovered. "I'm pretty sure they're VINs," I said.

"VINs?"

"Vehicle Identification Numbers. Every car has one. It's the number you use to register a car. It's what the police use to ID stolen cars." I knew because my dad had spent some time on the auto squad when he was a cop.

"If you're right, then you're lucky you didn't get caught—"

"I almost did." I told her what had happened with Phil Varton.

"That's too close for comfort, Robyn," she said with a shudder.

"You're telling me. I almost had a heart attack when Varton found me at my car. I thought he'd followed me."

Morgan apologized again for calling the police. "But when you didn't answer your phone, I was worried. So I called your dad's friend. I checked the card he gave you." I had stuck it to the fridge door. "I called him on his cell number, Robyn, you know, so that it was a personal thing, not a police thing. And I didn't tell him anything. I just said that you were out hiking, that you said something about taking photos out at that old church. He was in the middle of something, but he said he'd get someone to look into it for me. You don't think Phil Varton knew what you were doing out there, do you?"

"I don't know."

"So now what?"

"I'm going to call my dad again." I needed to hear his voice. I needed some advice.

"Sounds like a plan," Morgan said. "Let me know what happens."

I tried my dad, but I couldn't get through. I even tried my mom. Nothing. I stared out at the water and thought about what to do. Nick was right. Something was happening out there—and something else was going to happen tonight. What if Nick was involved? What if he was in danger?

I called Morgan back.

"What did your dad say?"

"I couldn't get hold of him."

"So now what?"

I stared out over the water to the Point, where I saw a tiny Morgan perched at the end of the dock, and I made up my mind.

"I'm going to do what my dad told me to do if anything came up," I said. "I'm going to talk to Chief Lafayette."

. . .

There were two police cars parked out front of the station, which meant Phil Varton was inside. I drew in a deep breath before I pushed open the door. A woman—a civilian—was working at a computer. Another civilian—a man—was on the phone. Phil Varton was at a desk on the far side of the room. He glanced at me as I entered the building. I went up to the woman at the computer and asked to speak to Chief Lafayette.

"I'm afraid he isn't—" she began.

Then a door opened behind me and a voice said, "Robyn!" Dean Lafayette looked happy, even relieved, to see me. I was just as relieved to see him.

"Can I talk to you for a minute?" I said.

"Certainly. What's up?"

"In private?" I said.

Dean Lafayette frowned, but he led me into a small, glassed-in office and closed the door. He invited me to take a seat, but I was too keyed up to sit.

"You look a little shaky, Robyn. Are you okay? Phil radioed me on his way back to town. He said he'd found you face-to-face with a bear. What were you doing out there in the first place?"

I hesitated. I knew it wasn't what Nick wanted me to do, but I had run out of options.

"I was out at the old sawmill on Larry Wilson's property. Something's going on out there. I'm not positive, but I think Mr. Wilson might be involved in a car-theft ring."

"What?" He looked stunned.

I told him everything I had told Morgan. I also told him my suspicions about Phil Varton.

His face went white.

"You actually saw Phil out there?" he said.

"Well, no. But I saw his gloves. And his car. That must be how he found me. He must have been right there when you radioed him."

Dean Lafayette shook his head and glanced through the glass at his deputy. "That's a pretty serious allegation, Robyn."

I looked out at Varton too. He was heading for the door. I relaxed a little when he left the building.

"I wouldn't be here if I wasn't sure," I said.

"I don't suppose you have any proof?"

"I took one of the VINs." I unshouldered my backpack and noticed, for the first time, that I hadn't zipped up some of the pockets. I reached into the one where I had put the VIN. It wasn't there. I checked the other pockets. Nothing. That couldn't be. I checked them again. The VIN was definitely missing.

"It must have fallen out," I said. "But I took pictures. Lots of them. My camera is in the car," I said. "I'll be right back."

I ran out of the station and across the road to my car in the marina parking lot. I was out of breath by the time I handed the camera over to Dean Lafayette back in his office.

He turned it on and looked into the display screen. He pressed the display button a few times. He was frowning when he looked up at me.

"There's nothing in here, Robyn."

"Sure there is. I took a dozen pictures, maybe more."
I took the camera from him and peered into the display
screen. Blank. I checked to see that the memory card was
still in the camera. It was.

"I don't understand," I said. "I took lots of pictures."

"Maybe you only thought you did," Dean Lafayette
said. "Maybe you pressed the wrong button. Is it a new
camera?"

"No. I borrowed it from my friend. But—"

"Not all cameras are the same. Maybe you—"

"I checked," I said. "I looked at the pictures when I
got back to my car."

Then it hit me: Varton had seen me looking at the
camera.

"Someone must have deleted them," I said.

"Someone? Who would do that?"

"Phil Varton."

I explained that I had put the camera in the glove
compartment for safekeeping. Phil Varton had seen me
do it. And he knew how to get into my car when it was
locked. I had seen him do that, too, when I'd left my keys
in the ignition.

Dean Lafayette leaned back in his chair and shook
his head. He looked extremely unhappy.

"I know what I saw out at Mr. Wilson's," I said. "And
he's the only person who could have done it."

"I believe you saw what you saw, Robyn," he said

slowly. "But Larry runs an auto-salvage business, and he's teaching those boys everything they need to know about auto repair. Maybe there's another explanation for what you saw."

"But what about the VINs?" I wished I'd remembered to zip up that pocket. "And those cars I saw out there—they weren't old clunkers that someone was selling for scrap or for parts. They looked almost new. And expensive. And if what Mr. Wilson is doing is legitimate, why is there so much activity going on there in the middle of the night?"

"Middle of the night? What are you talking about?"

I hesitated. I didn't want to break my promise to Nick.

"Remember when I ran into you at Roxy's and I asked you if you'd ever heard of anything strange going on out at Larry Wilson's place?" I said. "Well, I just got this odd feeling when I was out there. So I decided to watch the place one night."

"Watch the place?"

"To see if I was right."

He sighed. "You've put me in an awkward position here, Robyn."

"But I saw—"

"You've put me in an awkward position," he repeated. "You trespassed on private property. You have no proof of what you saw." He stood up. "But—I am going to look into it."

"But how? Don't you need a search warrant?"

He shook his head. "In addition to the group home, Larry Wilson runs a salvage operation out there. The county licenses salvage yards. It requires their owners to make themselves available for inspection at any time at the discretion of the chief of police. I can take a look around the whole property, and Larry can't stop me. If you're right, I'll find out about it."

Dean Lafayette's face was serious. He reminded me of my dad when he was getting to the bottom of something important.

"Unless he's been warned," I said. I kept thinking about Phil Varton.

"I'm going to pay Larry a surprise visit," he said. "If you're right, if Larry is up to something illegal out there and if Phil is in on it somehow, then there's no telling who else might be involved. Have you discussed this with anyone else? Anyone at the paper?"

I shook my head. "The only person I've talked to is my friend Morgan."

"Okay. Well, let's keep it that way until I have to chance to look into things. Okay?"

"Okay."

I left the police station and stood outside in the sun, wondering if I should have told him about Nick, too. But I decided I had done the right thing—at least I'd been able to keep Nick out of it. If Dean Lafayette was going to look into it, then Nick would be safe. As I headed back to the marina, I glanced into the police car in front of the police station. There was a pair of gloves on the passenger seat. One of the gloves had a grease stain on the index finger.

. . .

Colleen Duggan was outside the marina restaurant, writing the daily specials onto the menu board. I walked over to talk to her. When I had finished, I went back to my car. I knew I was right about everything I had seen, but Dean Lafayette was right too. I had no solid proof. If only I still had that VIN plate. It must have fallen out of my backpack, maybe when I ran into the bear, or when I threw my backpack into the car—or when I grabbed it again when I got out of the car. I was unlocking my door to take another look inside when my phone rang.

"Robyn?" said a whispery voice I didn't recognize.

"Who is this?"

"It's me," the voice said, so softly that I could hardly hear it. "Nick."

"Nick, I went out there like I said. I found—"

"I have to talk fast, Robyn, before someone catches me using the phone. You gotta be careful, okay? I was right. There's a cop involved."

"I know."

"Don't get involved, Robyn. I don't think—"

He broke off suddenly.

"Nick? Nick?"

"Someone's coming," he whispered. "I gotta go."

My heart was pounding again. I got into the car and

hunted for the VIN plate. But it wasn't on any of the seats or on the floor. That's when I realized that something else was missing. My notebook. I thought hard. I had left my camera in the glove compartment when I went down to the dock to call Morgan. But I had taken my backpack with me. It hadn't been out of my sight. And I clearly remembered putting the VIN plate into the pocket that held my notebook. But I hadn't zipped the pocket—I had been in too much of a rush to get out of the sawmill. Both the VIN plate and the notebook must have fallen out—maybe when I scrambled out of the building, or when I was hiding, or when I was climbing over the fence. If someone had found that notebook, they would know it was mine. They would know I had been there.

I was just about to get out of the car again when a shadow fell across the windshield. I stifled a scream when a face suddenly appeared. Phil Varton.

"Didn't mean to startle you," he said as I got out of the car. He was wearing his gloves again. I stared at them. Across the street, Dean Lafayette came out of the police station, got into his car, and drove away.

CHAPTER **FIFTEEN**

A couple hours later, I was standing under a window outside the marina restaurant, waiting for Morgan and gazing at the police station across the road. The air had turned cool, and clouds were building overhead. The breeze from the lake had turned into a sharp wind. Sometime tonight there would be rain. I checked my watch. Where was Morgan? Then I spotted her hobbling toward me. Her face was gleaming from exertion.

"Good news, Robyn," she called. She glanced up at the restaurant. "I'm so hungry," she said. "Let's go inside."

"First tell me the good news," I said. "Then we eat—my treat."

"Deal. Okay, so I e-mailed that guy I was telling you about, and he e-mailed me right back. He says he can do it, Robyn."

"He can restore the pictures in your camera?"

"Yes."

"Are you sure?"

"Yes, I'm sure. He says a lot of people assume that when they're gone, they're gone, no idea how to restore them. But he can do it. He's done it before, so there should be no problem. He's going to drive up here first thing tomorrow morning. As long as we have the camera—"

"We'll have it. It's in my glove compartment, and the car's locked. It'll be safe there," I said.

"Then you'll have the proof you need to—"

I clamped a hand over her mouth to silence her. "You did great, Morgan," I said. "Let's get something to eat."

We circled around to the front of the restaurant—and almost collided with Phil Varton, also on his way in. It was impossible to read his expression behind his mirrored sunglasses.

. . .

After we had stuffed ourselves on the daily special—fried chicken, followed by slices of homemade pie—we definitely needed our life jackets for the trip back to the Point. If either of us had fallen into the lake with all that food in our stomachs, we would have sunk like stones. The water was choppy, and we were shoved up and down as the boat sped over the crests of the scudding water. Morgan looked up at the threatening sky.

"There's going to be a storm," she said.

"Nothing like a little positive thinking," I said. But she was right.

We got home and sat in the kitchen, drinking tea. Billy called Morgan, and they chatted while I wondered how Nick was and what would happen tomorrow.

When Morgan finally ended her call, I checked all the doors and windows. I took another look at the sky, but it was impossible to see what was happening up there. The clouds hid the moon and the stars. I stared across the water, trying to see my car in the marina parking lot.

"It's going to be okay, Robyn," Morgan said. "You've done everything you can."

After all the excitement of the day, I was sure I wouldn't be able to sleep. I told myself to relax. I told myself that Morgan was right—I had done everything I could. The next day, if things went the way I hoped they would, everything would be okay.

· · ·

It wasn't the thunder that woke me up. It was the hand over my mouth. I kicked and struggled, but someone grabbed my arms and tied them behind my back. Someone else taped my mouth shut and slipped something over my head. Rough hands yanked me to my feet. I heard drawers opening and closing, and then more commotion down the hall as someone dragged me out of the bedroom. I tried again to break free, but the hands that were holding me were too strong. I was carried down the stairs, out of the house, and down to the dock. I felt the rain and wild wind on my skin. I was pushed into a boat. Judging from the thump that followed, so was Morgan. I heard a motor start. Then a second one. We started across the lake, the boat pounding up and down in the water.

It was impossible to tell how long the boat ride lasted—not that I was in any hurry to have it end. I was too afraid of what could happen when we got wherever we were going. I was shaking all over by the time we docked. I felt hands on me, half pushing, half lifting me.

The wind whipped through my thin pajamas. I shivered as I was shoved barefoot down the dock. A terrible thought struck me. What if I was being pushed to the end of the dock? What if they were going to throw me into the water? With my hands tied behind me, there would be nothing I could do.

I stumbled when I reached the end of the dock and made contact with land. I was nudged roughly along. I heard a door open and was pushed through it. I tripped and fell to the floor. Someone—Morgan—was thrust in after me. A door banged shut behind us. A voice said, "Robyn?"

Nick.

"Robyn, can you hear me?" His voice was low, but urgent.

I nodded my response.

"They've got me tied up," Nick said. "I'm over here."

I staggered toward his voice.

"That's it," he said, encouraging me. "A little closer. A little closer."

I felt something warm and firm. Nick's arm.

"Go behind me. I think I can get your blindfold off."

I maneuvered around him and knelt down so that he could grab the hood on my head. Once he had a grip on it, I pulled free, and there was Nick, his hands tied behind his back.

"I think I can get that tape off," he said. "But it might hurt."

I positioned my face near his hands and almost started to cry when I felt his fingers touch my cheek. He picked at a corner of the tape until he worked it free.

"Okay," he said. "Here goes."

With one quick jerk, he ripped the tape from my mouth. He was right. It hurt—a lot. But I didn't care. I staggered to my feet and peered into the gloom.

"Morgan," I said.

With her foot in a cast, Morgan had more trouble getting around. I went to her and pulled off her hood with my teeth. Her eyes were frantic. I went to work on the tape that covered her mouth.

"What happened?" she said when I finally tore off the tape. "Who were those people? Where are we?"

"Larry and some of his guys," Nick said. "They grabbed me a couple of hours ago. I heard them say your name, Robyn, but there was nothing I could do to warn you." He sounded angry. "I never should have got you involved."

"So much for that plan," Morgan said.

"What plan?" Nick said.

"You said they would just take the camera," Morgan said. "You said that's all we needed to prove—"

"I was wrong," I said. I felt terrible.

"What plan?" Nick said.

I filled him in on the scheme Morgan and I had cooked up. Then, before he could quiz me, I said, "Do you know where we are, Nick?"

He shook his head. "I wasn't able to see where they were taking me."

"What do you think they're going to do with us?" Morgan asked, her voice trembling.

"I don't know."

"Robyn, let me see if I can untie your hands," Nick said.

I went back to Nick and stood with my back to his. His fingers slid against my skin as he worked to untie the knots in my rope.

"Jeez," he said, "must have been tied by a Boy Scout."

"You were right about the sawmill," I said. "There's a car-theft ring out there."

"You saw something?"

I described everything, including the police car and the gloved hand.

"We've got to get out of here," Nick said. He fumbled with the knots, but he wasn't getting anywhere. "Did you talk to Ed Jarvis?" he said. "Did you find out anything about the guys who ran away from here?"

"Only that there's no record of where they are now. And . . ."

"And what?"

"Neither of them had any family. They were just like that kid Steven who ran away—the one they found out in the woods."

There was complete silence in the room for a moment. After a few somber moments, Nick said, "Alex was different. He had a family. He had Seth. If Alex had run away, Seth would have done something. He loved that kid, Robyn. As sick as he was, he would have done something to find him."

I heard Morgan sniffling softly behind me.

"We can't just disappear, Morgan," I said. "Nobody would believe that we would run away and never contact anyone we knew ever again. Nobody would believe that we would commit suicide, either."

"We get kidnapped in the middle of the night, and you're trying to tell me nothing bad is going to happen to us?"

"Shhhh," Nick said. "I heard something."

We all fell silent. It was the sound of a car, and it was coming toward us.

"Ohmygod," Morgan whimpered. "Ohmygod."

I heard a car door open and then slam shut again, then footsteps coming toward us. The lock on the door rattled.

The door opened, and in the moonlight I saw Dean Lafayette.

CHAPTER SIXTEEN

Dean Lafayette flipped a switch inside the door, turning on a single lightbulb suspended from a cord overhead. He was wearing gloves. There was an oil stain on one of them.

He came into the room, turned me around, removed the gloves, and started to untie my hands. A shadow fell across the floor. I gasped. It was Larry Wilson. He was flanked by Derek and Bruno and another guy whom I didn't recognize. Everyone except Wilson was holding a gun.

Dean Lafayette turned to face them.

"You were supposed to just take the camera, not the girls. Without those pictures, they've got nothing," he said.

"They know too much," Wilson said. "You said yourself she was out at the sawmill. You think she's going to keep quiet about that?"

"For God's sake, I know her father," Dean Lafayette said. "I've known him for twenty years."

"And he's an ex-cop. And a PI. You think she won't tell him? You think he'd let a thing like this go?"

"I know he won't let a thing like his daughter's death go."

Death? I glanced at Morgan. She had turned ash-gray.

"Two girls who don't know any better take a boat out and get caught in a storm. These things happen," Wilson said.

Dean Lafayette stared at him for a moment. Then he freed my hands. I felt a surge of hope. He inspected my wrists.

"You're lucky there are no bruises or rope marks," he said. He gestured to Nick. "What about him?"

"What about him?" Wilson echoed. "He's just a kid who's going to disappear—a runaway, like the others."

Dean Lafayette shook his head. "I don't like it. That's four deaths."

Four? Who was the fourth?

"*Two*," Wilson said. "Two accidental deaths. One disappearance. One runaway. And you'll be in charge of the investigation. Relax, Dean."

The two men locked eyes.

"Okay," Lafayette said. "But it had better be convincing."

"I'm sure you'll see to that," Wilson said.

"Me? I'm having no part—"

"You're coming with us," Wilson said. "You're

helping. That way you won't be tempted to rat us out."

Dean Lafayette tensed all over. Bruno gestured with the gun in his hand, and Dean Lafayette raised his arms just high enough to let Derek relieve him of his weapon.

"Good," Wilson said. "Now, let's get this over with." He turned to Bruno. "Untie the other girl's hands, too. Dean's right. If it's going to look like an accident, we don't want any bruises on their wrists. And see that they get dressed."

"Get up," Bruno said to Morgan. He yanked her to her feet. She let out a yelp, but he didn't care that he was hurting her. I kicked him hard. He doubled over, groaning. Derek pointed his gun at Nick.

"You make another move like that and he dies," he said. "I mean it."

I glanced at Nick. He shook his head. Larry Wilson threw a plastic bag at my feet.

"Get dressed," he said.

Morgan looked at me in horror. Being kidnapped was terrifying. But from the look on her face, the thought of dressing in front of all these men was even scarier.

"Can we at least have a little privacy?" I said.

Wilson nodded.

"Over there," Derek said, his gun on us.

There was a small stack of wooden crates. If we stood behind them, we could dress in relative modesty.

"You try anything, Nick's the first to get it," Derek said.

I untied Morgan, and we dressed as quickly as we

could with shaking hands. Then they led us back out to the dock and onto a boat. The rain was pelting down, and lightning flashed across the sky. Derek got into the boat first and held his gun on us while we followed. Someone shoved me down some steps into the boat's small cabin, where I tripped over something—a body. Phil Varton.

Morgan slammed into me and crashed to the floor. Then Nick stumbled in. The door slammed behind him, and I heard the click of a lock turning.

"My ankle," Morgan moaned. "I think I broke it again."

I rushed to her.

"Let me see, Morgan." She cringed when I touched her ankle. The cast was wet but seemed okay otherwise. I glanced at Nick. I knew he was thinking the same thing that I was: the pain in her ankle was nothing compared to what was going to happen next. Nick knelt down beside Phil Varton.

"He's still alive," he said. He bent down to look more closely at him. "He's chained, Robyn. Weights on him, too."

They were planning to throw him overboard. Weighted down, he would never be found. I had no doubt that Dean Lafayette would have some story to explain his absence.

"What about us? What are they going to do?" Morgan said in a small voice.

More chains lay on the floor beside Phil Varton. I felt sick when I realized they were for Nick.

We were racing farther and farther from shore. The boat was bouncing up and down on the mounting waves.

"I'm going to untie Nick's hands." I talked softly to her, the way I would to a scared little kid. "Okay?"

She nodded.

As I worked on the ropes around Nick's wrists, Nick said, "They'll probably take Varton as far out as they can and sink him deep. You and Morgan . . ." The rope fell from his wrists. "You heard what he said, Robyn. You saw it. They're towing Morgan's boat. They're probably going to make it look like you two were out in the storm, maybe ran out of gas, or something went wrong with the engine, maybe you decided to try for shore—"

Morgan whimpered.

I looked around. We were in a small cabin. There were windows all around us, but they were too small to squeeze through even if we could get them open. And there was a door—just one.

"We could stop them from coming in," I said.

"They have guns," Morgan said in a shaky voice.

"They want it to look like an accident," I pointed out. "They want our bodies to be found. They don't want our parents"—my dad—"poking around up here."

Nick squeezed my hand.

"These guys are serious, Robyn. Four kids are dead already. If we give them any trouble, they'll just shoot us, at least shoot one of us, and weight us down, too, so no one will ever find us."

"There has to be something we can do," I said, more

for Morgan's sake than because I believed it.

Phil Varton groaned. His eyes fluttered open and then closed again. I went to him. His hair was matted with blood. I could see the rise and fall of his chest, but I had no idea how badly he was hurt.

"They're eventually gonna come and get us," Nick said. "Our only chance is to get into the water before they can do anything to us."

"Jump overboard, you mean?" I said.

Nick nodded grimly.

"Morgan can't swim with that cast on," I said.

"I don't know what else to do, Robyn," Nick said. "They're gonna kill us. We can't just let them do it without a fight."

"But they have guns . . ."

"You have a better idea?"

Outside, the wind roared. The small boat pitched and rolled. I heard someone shout but couldn't make out what he was saying.

Then the boat slowed.

The door to the cabin opened. Bruno appeared, swaying in the doorway.

"Up," he said. "Now."

"See if you can grab some life jackets," Nick whispered. "The first chance you two have, get into the water." He staggered to his feet. I reached for Morgan to help her up.

Morgan moaned. Her face was pale with pain.

"Come on, Morgan." I leaned in close to her. "We

have to at least try."

Phil Varton groaned again. Bruno grabbed me and shoved me out onto the deck. Derek was out there.

"Watch her," Bruno told him.

Derek forced me down onto the deck and held a gun on me. I looked up and saw Dean Lafayette at the wheel. Larry Wilson was standing beside him. The boat came to a stop. Dean Lafayette started toward the stern. He was the only one of the three who was wearing a life jacket.

Nick stumbled out onto the deck. Bruno was right behind him. He forced Nick down to his knees.

Dean Lafayette left Wilson at the wheel and started coming toward me. I turned to Nick. His eyes went to Lafayette. Bruno shoved Morgan roughly up the steps onto the deck. She stumbled and cried out in pain. Derek grabbed her, yanked her to her feet, and pushed her out onto the deck. Then he turned to Dean Lafayette.

"Get their boat," he said. "Get ready."

Nick was still kneeling on the deck, but his eyes were hard on Bruno. His whole body was rigid. He nodded. Then everything happened at once.

A huge wave slammed into the boat, and it rocked violently. Nick was on his hands and knees now, drenched. His eyes still focused on Bruno, Nick surged upward. He slammed into Bruno and knocked the gun from his hand. Derek grabbed Morgan and threw her against the side of the boat, out of his way. He raised his gun and aimed it at Nick. Nick swung around, taking Bruno with him so that Bruno was between Nick and Derek. At that same instant, Derek fired.

Nick fell backward into the water, still holding Bruno. Derek rushed to the rail and fired again. Another wave crashed against the boat. Morgan screamed. I watched in horror as she was swept into the water. I started for the side of the boat but stopped when Derek swung his gun around at me. It looked as big as a cannon.

Out of the corner of my eye I saw Dean Lafayette reach behind himself. I saw his arm come around again. He swung it at Derek.

A shot rang out.

Derek collapsed on the deck.

I turned and stared at Dean Lafayette. He looked at me for a second, then spun around and headed back to Larry Wilson at the wheel. Wilson turned to escape, but Lafayette tackled him from behind and crashed with him to the deck. A moment later, Lafayette was on his feet again. He hauled Wilson up off the deck. I saw the flash of handcuffs. Then Dean Lafayette worked his way back over the heaving deck to me.

I heard Morgan cry out, "Help!"

"There's a searchlight up there," Dean Lafayette yelled over the roar of the storm. "Turn it on. See if you can find your friends." He grabbed a couple of life jackets and dove over the side of the boat into the black, roiling water.

I scrambled up the steps to where the steering wheel was. The boat was pitching and tossing even more violently. I lost my balance and slammed against the wheel. It took me a moment to regain my footing and make my way to the light. I swept the beam across the water and saw nothing but waves and blackness. No Nick. No Morgan. I called their names, but the wind seemed to whip the words right back at me.

I swept the water again, more slowly this time, forcing myself to look carefully. Then:

"There," I screamed into the wind. "Starboard side," I shouted to Dean Lafayette. "I see something on the starboard side."

A hand. The side of a face. A mass of chestnut hair—Morgan's current color. Then nothing.

"Morgan," I screamed. "Morgan, hold on."

Morgan had taken swimming lessons with Billy and me every year when we were younger. I knew she could swim. But for the past couple of years she had been enjoying sitting on the dock more than fooling around in the water. "I don't want to mess up my hair" was her standard excuse. I hoped she hadn't lost her strength, or that she could at least manage to tread water. The lake was choppy. The waves were high. And she had a cast on her leg.

I kept the light on the place where I had last seen her. Dean Lafayette doggedly swam toward the focused beam. A hand broke through the surface. I shouted. Lafayette grabbed the hand and pulled. I held my breath. Morgan's head emerged from the water, and Dean Lafayette pulled her to him. Her eyes were closed.

I couldn't tell if she was breathing or not. He slipped a life jacket on her and started to tow her back toward the boat. With every stroke he took, the wind and the waves seemed to push him two strokes farther away. *Please*, I prayed. *Please.*

Finally he was within a few feet of the side of the boat. I raced down the steps just as his hand grabbed the gunwale. I caught hold of Morgan's life jacket and held tight while Dean Lafayette clambered aboard. Together we hauled her out of the water and onto the deck. Dean Lafayette immediately laid her down on the deck and pressed a finger against her neck to check for a pulse. He tipped her head back to open her airway and began mouth-to-mouth resuscitation.

"What about Nick?" I said.

"You know how to do this?"

"Yes."

He moved aside so that I could take over, then scrambled back up to the light and swept the water.

I tried to focus on Morgan. I pinched her nose lightly and breathed into her mouth until I saw her chest rise. *Come on, Morgan. Come on.* I felt myself start to panic. She had been in the water for a few minutes, but I had no idea how long she had been submerged. It was all my fault. None of this would have happened if it weren't for me. And what about Nick? Where was he?

Don't think about that, Robyn. Morgan needs your help. She needs you to stay calm. Breathe out and watch Morgan's lungs expand, one, two. Release and watch them fall, two, three, four. Breathe, count, release, count.

Dean Lafayette swept the water and called out Nick's name.

Morgan spluttered. I rolled her over onto her side and let her cough out the water. Lafayette had abandoned his search. He jumped down onto the deck and knelt down to see how Morgan was.

"I don't have a phone," he said. "And there's no radio on board. We have to go back. We have to get to a phone and call emergency rescue."

"But Nick—"

"I can't see him, Robyn," he said. "No sign of Bruno, either. In this storm, they could be anywhere. We have to go back. The faster we do that, the better chance Nick has. Robyn, Morgan needs your help. She needs to get out of those wet clothes. So do you."

He dug in his pocket for something—a key. "The two of you get in the cabin. Get out of those clothes. There are some blankets down there. Then help Phil. Here's the key to his chains."

"But I—"

"Now, Robyn."

Tears burned my eyes as I helped Morgan down into the cabin. She was coughing, and her lips were turning blue. She was trembling all over. I helped her to sit down, then tore open cupboards and drawers until I found a couple of old sweaters and some blankets. I helped Morgan peel off her damp clothes and pull a sweater over her head. I wrapped her in a blanket. I did the same for myself. Then I knelt down beside Phil Varton and undid the lock that held him chained. His eyes were open.

"Are you all right?" I said.

Slowly he raised a hand and touched it to his head. He looked groggy as he struggled to a seated position.

Once I was sure that he and Morgan were going to be okay, I went back out on deck. We were headed for the marina. I could see its lights flash off and on above the waves. When we got close enough, I saw two figures on the dock—Al Duggan and his daughter Colleen. Dean Lafayette tossed a line to Al and another one to Colleen, and they pulled us in to the dock.

"Help them," he said to Al Duggan as he jumped off the boat. He said something else to Duggan that I couldn't hear. Then he sprinted up to the marina restaurant.

CHAPTER SEVENTEEN

Al Duggan led us to the house behind the marina restaurant. He phoned someone—a doctor who lived nearby. While we waited for him, Colleen gave Morgan and me some dry clothes to wear. Duggan made Phil Varton lie down on the sofa. The doctor came and checked us all over. He told Al Duggan that both Phil Varton and Morgan should go to the hospital—Varton needed an X-ray and stitches in his head. Morgan also needed an X-ray to make sure that there was no further damage to her ankle. Duggan said that he would take them right away.

"Come with me, Robyn," Morgan said. "Please. You can't do anything here."

"What about Nick?" I said.

"When they find him, someone will tell us."

I could have hugged her for saying *when*. Still, I was reluctant to go. But Morgan insisted.

． ． ．

The sun was coming up by the time Morgan appeared in a wheelchair pushed by an orderly. She had a brand-new cast on her ankle and a new set of crutches.

"I called your parents," I said. "They're on their way up. They want you to call them as soon as you can."

"Any word on Nick?"

I shook my head and fought back tears. "I haven't heard anything at all."

I wheeled Morgan to the emergency waiting room. When we got there, Morgan called her parents and they told her to stay where she was. They said they'd be there within the hour.

"Are you okay?" I asked Morgan.

"My ankle got re-broken," she said. "I've got to have this cast on for six more weeks. There goes my whole summer." She gave me a sheepish look. "You know what I mean."

I put an arm around her. When everything else was completely crazy, I could always count on Morgan to be Morgan.

"I wish I knew what was going on," I said. "I wish I knew where Nick was."

Morgan squeezed my hand.

The emergency department doors parted and a gurney rolled in, pushed by two ambulance attendants. There was a doctor alongside it, checking on the patient.

I saw a shock of black hair. Walking beside the gurney was a police officer, Detective Goyer. The police had sent him to take over the investigation. He'd already arrested Dean Lafayette, Derek, and Larry Wilson. He had questioned me while Morgan was being treated.

I stood up and ran to the gurney.

Nick.

He was wrapped in a blanket. His hair was wet and matted. And the scar on his face stood out against the whiteness of his face.

"Nick!"

He managed a faint smile.

One of the ambulance attendants asked me to stand back, and they whisked Nick away down the hall. I started after him, but Detective Goyer grabbed my arm.

"He was shot," he said.

"Shot?" Derek had fired at Nick just before he went into the water with Bruno.

"It's a flesh wound. In and out on his left arm. He's going to be okay, but he needs medical attention," Goyer said. "How's your friend?"

"She's fine," I said. "Her parents are on their way up here."

. . .

While Nick was being taken care of, Morgan and I went over our story again for Detective Goyer.

"Nick is the one who figured out that something

wasn't right out there," I said. "He tipped me off that there was a police officer involved."

"But how did he know that?" Morgan asked.

"He overheard Wilson and Bruno talking," Detective Goyer said. "Apparently Wilson had been hinting around that he could help Nick make money. Bruno wasn't sure about Nick—he kept pressing Wilson. He said Wilson's cop friend should use his contacts to check up on him."

"I'm glad he didn't get around to it," I said. "He might have found out that Nick knew me. And my dad." I thought about Phil Varton. "I was so sure Officer Varton was the cop who was involved. He seemed to be watching Larry's guys all the time."

"He was," Goyer said. "He said he had a feeling there was something wrong out there. Every now and then he'd see lights on in the area, in the middle of nowhere. When that happened, he said, he would swing by the next day and ask Wilson about it, but Wilson always said he had no idea what Varton was talking about. Varton offered to check it out for him, but Wilson never took him up on it." Goyer shook his head. "He also reported it to Lafayette, but all he ever said was that Wilson was doing good work out there and that the police should be supporting him. He never let Varton do an inspection. You did good work, Robyn, figuring out what was going on and Lafayette's part in it."

"And all over a stain on a glove," Morgan said. "I'm impressed."

"Well, Colleen helped," I admitted.

"Right. She saw Lafayette break into your car at the marina," Morgan said.

"Not exactly. She saw him near my car while I was on the phone, and I kind of assumed the rest. Those pictures were there when I left my camera in the glove compartment—and I was watching Lafayette when he looked at my camera and said they were gone. They must have been deleted before then. When I came out of the station after talking to him, I saw those gloves in the police car—the ones with the stain on them. I'd been sure they were Officer Varton's. But I talked to Colleen and found out that the chief, not Varton, had been poking around my car. Then I realized that not only had I lost the VIN plate from the sawmill, I had also lost my notebook. I'd put them both into the same pocket of my backpack. But I had my backpack with me the whole time, which meant I must have dropped them out by the sawmill.

"A few minutes after I talked to Colleen, Varton approached me in the marina parking lot. He was wearing gloves, but they weren't the ones I'd seen out at the sawmill—no stain on them. Then I saw Lafayette come out of the police station and get into the same car where I'd seen the gloves. That's when it all came together. It was Lafayette who had been near my car. The gloves I had seen were his. I thought, what if he'd found the VIN plate and the notebook that I dropped out at the sawmill?"

"He did," Detective Goyer said. "We found the

notebook partially burned in a fire pit out behind his house. He knew you'd been out there before you went to talk to him."

"That's what I was thinking," I said. "And Officer Varton told him when he radioed in that he'd found me taking pictures out there. While I was talking to Morgan out on the dock, Lafayette broke into my car and deleted all the pictures."

"I still don't understand why he didn't just steal the camera," Morgan said.

"Maybe he thought that would look more suspicious," I said.

"Well it's a good thing that Morgan knew that those images could be restored," Goyer said. Morgan and I exchanged glances. The truth was that Morgan didn't know anyone who could restore images on the memory card of a digital camera. Neither of us had a clue whether it was even possible to restore images in the first place. It was a bluff.

"We made sure Lafayette overheard us saying that someone was coming up the next day to restore the pictures so that we'd have proof. Colleen had told us he always came into her family's restaurant on Tuesdays for the fried chicken, so we got her to seat him near a window." I said. "We knew he or someone else would want to get that camera before Morgan's friend got here. And we knew if we could catch them, we'd have proof that something was going on."

"And it really was a car-theft ring?" Morgan said.

Goyer nodded.

"Chopping and stripping mostly," he said.

Morgan frowned. "Chopping and stripping?"

"Chopping is when thieves dismantle a car so they can sell the parts to legitimate and illegitimate body shops," he explained. "Stripping's similar. Some car-theft rings ship parts overseas, where the cars are reassembled and sold. Or they strip a car and then abandon it. The owner, of course, calls the police and reports the car abandoned. When the police eventually find the stripped car, the theft record is canceled. The car's useless to the owner, who claims insurance. Then the car is sold at an insurance auction. The thieves purchase the frame, supposedly for salvage, reattach the stolen parts, and sell the car, which is no longer listed as stolen. They put fake or stolen VINs in them so that they can be registered."

"And he was recruiting kids to get involved," I said grimly.

"We talked to some of the other kids out there," Detective Goyer said. "Some of them refused to say a word. But some seemed relieved to be able to talk about it. Every single one of those kids is on his own, just like your friend Nick. They have nowhere else to turn, nowhere they really belong."

"Just like Steven," Morgan said.

"And Lucas," I said. "He told Nick he was glad when the cops showed up in town, that he wanted to get arrested and sent back to the city. He said he didn't want to get involved in anything illegal, but Wilson was pressuring him. It got so bad that he decided he would rather end up doing time for year or two if it meant he could get away from Larry."

"What about Alex Richmond?" Morgan said. "Was he really a suicide?"

"We don't know yet," Detective Goyer said. "Lafayette denies any involvement. Wilson isn't talking and, so far, Derek is in no shape to tell us anything."

CHAPTER **EIGHTEEN**

When Morgan's parents arrived they engulfed her in hugs. They embraced me, too, and wanted to take us back to the city immediately.

"Robyn can't go until Nick is released," Morgan said.

I told them it was okay, they should leave without me, but they wouldn't hear of it. Morgan's father got coffee for everyone, and we sat in the waiting room until a doctor finally told us that they were going to discharge Nick. They brought him out in a wheelchair. His arm was in a sling. The doctor explained to him that he would have to either see his own doctor as soon as possible or come back to the hospital to get his dressing changed and have someone look at the wound. Morgan's mom, who had never met Nick, stepped forward to listen to the instructions from the doctor.

We drove back to the city with Morgan's parents. Morgan had taken some painkillers and fell asleep almost immediately. Nick put his good arm around me and held me close. We didn't say anything, not with Morgan's parents right there. We were halfway home when Morgan's father's phone rang. It was my dad, sounding anxious and wanting to know if Morgan's parents had talked to Morgan recently. Morgan's mom handed me the phone.

"Robbie, thank God," my dad said. "I've been trying to get you for more than twenty-four hours. You can't imagine what I was thinking."

"Where are you, Dad?"

"At the airport. I'll be home tomorrow. Are you two having a good time?"

I glanced at Nick.

"We're on our way back to the city, Dad. I'll see you tomorrow."

. . .

Morgan's parents wanted me to go home with them, but I didn't want to leave Nick, and I knew that Nick wouldn't be comfortable with strangers. Morgan argued with them, and they finally, reluctantly, dropped Nick and me at my dad's building. We went up to my dad's place, and I got Nick settled in my dad's bed.

"Does it hurt?" I asked.

"Yeah," he said. "Guys in movies take a bullet and all they do is grimace. But it hurts way more than that."

"I thought you drowned."

"I thought I would. I knew I was shot, but I didn't

know how bad. And Bruno kept holding onto me. I don't think he knew how to swim. I tried, Robyn—"

"He tried to kill you."

He looked at me with his purple eyes. "I'm not like him, Robyn. I couldn't just let him drown. But . . ." He shook his head, and I saw real regret on his face.

I laid down on the bed beside him and put my head on his chest.

.   .   .

Someone shook me gently.

"Robbie?"

I opened my eyes and looked around. Nick was sound asleep beside me, and my dad was standing over me, looking fatherly and concerned. I slipped off the bed and tiptoed to the door. Dad followed me. I closed the door quietly behind me.

"You want to explain?" my dad said.

My father made coffee and toast, and we sat in the living room, where I told him everything that had happened over the past few weeks.

"You should have told me," he said.

"This was important to Nick, Dad."

My dad sat back in his chair and looked at me. "What are you going to tell your mother? She'll be back in a couple of days."

"I don't know."

. . .

Two days later we were in my dad's car, headed north. Nick sat in the back. His arm was still in a sling and he was still taking painkillers, but the color had come back into his face. We'd heard from Goyer—Alex Richmond had drowned, but it hadn't been an accident. He had been murdered. Derek had made a deal. He'd told the police everything. Nick had broken the news to Seth.

Steven, it turned out, had really died of exposure.

Dean Lafayette had confessed his part in the car-theft ring—he made sure that Larry Wilson and his gang were never hassled. But he claimed that he didn't know anything about the deaths of Larry's kids and told the police that he drew the line at murder.

"Do you think that's true?" I asked my dad.

He couldn't answer.

We were going back because Nick wanted to help make the case against Wilson. He intended to give the police as much information as he could to make sure that Alex's murderers paid for what they had done. I was going back to my job.

As we passed the sign that welcomed us to town, Dad put a hand on mine. He glanced at Nick.

"Are you two sure this is what you want to do?" he said.

I looked over my shoulder at Nick. "Yes," I said. "We are."

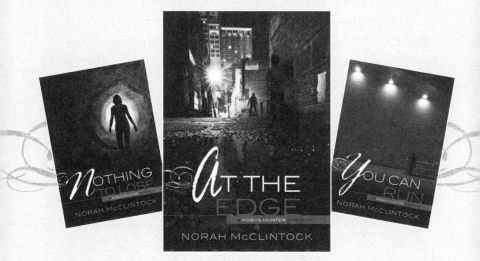
I arrived in the kitchen just in time to see James, soaking wet, dash back into the house. He peeled off his sodden T-shirt. A huge scar ran diagonally across his back, deep reddish-purple. Then I heard his father's voice, hard and sharp. "I told you I never wanted to see that thing again," he snarled. "It's bad enough that he's dead and that it's your fault . . ."

#1 Last Chance

Robyn's scared of dogs—but she agrees to spend time at an animal shelter anyway. Robyn learns that many juvenile offenders also volunteer at the shelter—including Nick D'Angelo. Nick has a talent for troublemaking, but after his latest arrest, Robyn suspects that he might be innocent. And she sets out to prove it . . .

#2 You Can Run

Trisha Hanover has run away from home before. But this time, she hasn't come back. To make matters worse, Robyn blew up at Trisha the same morning she disappeared. Now Robyn feels responsible, and she decides to track Trisha down . . .

#3 Nothing to Lose

Robyn is excited to hang out with Nick after weeks apart. She's sure he has reformed—until she notices suspicious behavior during their trip to Chinatown. Turns out Nick's been doing favors for dangerous people. Robyn urges him to stop, but the situation might be out of her control—and Nick's . . .

#4 Out of the Cold

Robyn's friend Billy drags her into volunteering at a homeless shelter. When one of the shelter's regulars freezes to death on a harsh winter night, Robyn wonders if she could've prevented it. She sets out to find about more about the man's past, and discovers unexpected danger in the process . . .

#5 *Shadow of Doubt*

Robyn's new substitute teacher Ms. Denholm is cool, pretty, and possibly the target of a stalker. When Denholm receives a threatening package, Robyn wonders who's responsible. But Robyn has a mystery of her own to worry about: What's with the muddled phone message she receives from her missing ex-boyfriend Nick?

#6 *Nowhere to Turn*

Robyn has sworn that she's over Nick. But when she hears he needs help, she's too curious about why he went missing to say no. Nick has been arrested again, and the evidence doesn't lean in his favor. When Robyn investigates, she discovers a situation more complicated than the police had thought—and more deadly. . .

#7 *Change of Heart*

Robyn's best friend Billy has been a mess ever since her *other* best friend Morgan dumped him. To make matters worse, Morgan started dating hockey star Sean Sloane right afterward. Billy is an animal rights activist—he wouldn't hurt a fly. But when Sean winds up dead, can Robyn prove Billy's innocence?

#8 In Too Deep

Robyn should be having the time of her life. She has a great summer job and a room in Morgan's lake house. But suddenly Nick appears in town—on a mission. He promised a friend he'd investigate a local suicide. Did Alex Richmond drown himself? Or was he killed because he knew too much?

#9 At the Edge

Robyn just wants to spend time with Nick, but he's always busy. Morgan thinks James Derrick, a hot transfer student, could take Nick off her mind. But James has problems of his own. When Robyn realizes she and James share a hidden connection, she starts to dig deeper. But is she digging her own grave?

ABOUT THE AUTHOR

Norah McClintock is the author of several mystery series
for teenagers and a five-time winner of the Crime Writers of
Canada's Arthur Ellis Award for Best Juvenile Crime Novel.
McClintock was born and raised in Montreal, Quebec. She lives
in Toronto with her husband and children.